F JOH

IF I DIE TELL STEVE MARTIN I FOUND HIS JOURNAL

This is a work of fiction. Names, characters, places, and incidents either are products of the author's imagination or are used fictitiously. Any resemblance to actual events, or persons, living or dead, is entirely coincidental.

www.BillyJohnson.co
info@BillyJohnson.co

PUBLICITY AND MEDIA
Steve Flynn
Langdon-Flynn Communications
2760 Lake Sahara Drive
Las Vegas, NV
702-889-2705

IF I DIE TELL STEVE MARTIN I FOUND HIS JOURNAL
A Novel by Billy Johnson
Edited by Lisa Ferguson
Cover and book design by Billy Johnson
Photography by Jerry Gallegos, IIA Photography

FIRST EDITION

Copyright © 2013 Billy Johnson
All rights reserved.
ISBN-10: 0989682102
ISBN-13: 978-0-989-6821-0-7

for Loretta

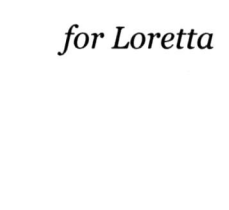

"Let us just say I was deeply unhappy,
but I didn't know it because I was so happy all the time."

Harris K. Telemacher

CONTENTS

	Prologue	1
1.	Found	7
2.	Frozen	35
3.	Beached	53
4.	Barstools	83
5.	Clocks	99
6.	Animal Rescue	119
7.	Cindy, et al	139
8.	Translation	163
9.	Oblivion	179
10.	Fate	201
11.	Imported Beer	225
12.	Death & Life	245
13.	Unscrambled	263
14.	Discovery	273
15.	Chance	283

PROLOGUE

SIX-HUNDRED PEOPLE, divided into groups of eight and seated at round tables, threw adoring gazes toward the dais as Navin reached the microphone. The charisma that shot from his sky-blue eyes dared all to be anything but indifferent toward his acceptance speech. A pause, a glare and a reputation drew anticipatory chuckles.

Navin sneered down at Simon, the portly president of the North American Marketing and Public Relations Society seated at Table One, and rolled his eyes. He filled his cheeks with air and held his breath.

Simon fidgeted and giggled until his fat belly shook. Spider veins in his cheeks grew violet, and an artery rose from his neck. Navin knew by Simon's obvious unease that Simon knew he was screwed.

Navin looked to the ground, and then released the air

through his nose, filling the speakers with the sound of a prolonged, wind-blasted rumble. He ignored the microphone and spoke to the floor. "They said there'd be cash," he said to an eruption of laughter and applause. He froze until the outburst grew silent then swelled into a second wave of laughter that crashed toward him. "Cash," Navin said. He raised his eyes back to Simon. "They said there'd be cash."

Simon's laughter was swallowed up by that of the room's. Navin's stern stare released into a subtle grin, which relieved Simon from what could have become a merciless roast.

The room settled and Navin explained how a call from midnight last tricked him into flying to New York in time for the event. He was to attend tonight, he said, to meet with the brass of a telecommunications company that had a "sticky messaging challenge." But there was no such company, just a bunch of "lowlife marketing types" to honor their "deserving king."

Navin owned fame as an innovative spin doctor with an offbeat, biting wit. His reputation made funny things he said unbearable and hilarious items murderous.

His insights brought worship. They were often technically correct counterculture viewpoints. His advice was the yield from a rebellious mindset. In groups such as this, the character he played to mask his fear of attention was reluctantly captivating.

His averseness was on display in the way he dressed: unfashionable blue jeans, a limp-collared shirt, scuffed shoes and a pilled sport coat. He was stylish by accident.

His blonde locks flew in several directions to form an air of apathy. But to admirers, all this—combined with an unshaven face—made him appear a maverick.

His acceptance speech, which was ad-libbed because he had been misled into attending, reminded many of the logic he turned into spin and marketing gold. His logic had afforded him an adequate financial autonomy, largely because he repelled a life of excess. But somewhere in his mid-thirties, just a handful of years ago, he grew unmotivated and began to shut everything down. His mind—the only real product he had to sell—grew tinged with intolerance and lethargy but, ironically, became ever more valuable to corporate America. He was increasingly described as "fresh" and "critical," even "important." As he tried less, he earned more.

"Nobody uses orange as a color," Navin once said dismissively to an investment firm. Months later, the firm's new orange identity pulled its brand from obscurity.

He convinced a fledgling energy drink company to commit to giving free product to the nation's third-largest fast-food chain for five years. "Let them sell it and keep the profits," he said. They did, and the drink company grew to rank second in annual retail sales within thirty-six months.

His value wasn't limited to generating revenue: A major automobile manufacturer slithered from a massive class-action suit. A particular model, the Grabber hatchback, had a propensity to put itself into gear. Gas stations and drive-in bank teller lanes were venues for a number of deaths and injuries.

"The emergency brake is called an emergency brake for a reason," Navin said. "It is listed as such in the owner's manual, yes?" This insight was worth nearly a quarter-billion dollars.

On the strength of this lore, Navin became a reluctant giant within a massive sphere—a sphere that had been reduced on this day to six hundred or so businessmen and women who represented the countless who toil over laptop computers to reduce <u>War and Peace</u> to a manipulative thirty-second sound bite. But giants remain unconquerable if they can't be reached. And Navin, the loner, was as aloof as he was talented.

Throughout his speech, Navin was grateful and sweet. He was cynical and logical. Terse and poignant. And throughout, he was funny. As the belly of the room burned from laughter, Navin closed his remarks. He concluded in a fashion short of cryptic, but nevertheless in a manner missed by all. "Never meet your heroes," he said. "They'll only let you down."

He thanked them and said goodbye. People stood and applauded. He graciously shook the hands of those who honored him, flung his coat over his forearm and escaped through the room's back door.

As he flowed through a labyrinth of service hallways, past kitchens and other empty conference rooms, he unfolded his coat and put it on, left arm first, without ever breaking stride. He emptied his pockets of a scarf, hat and gloves. He bundled and buttoned quickly, as he walked with the purpose of a fireman donning his gear while the idling fire engine waited and the station's garage doors were opening.

He spotted an illuminated sign that read "EXIT" and burst through a steel door that spit him into a frozen Manhattan bathed by a blinding sun. Within minutes, he found the book that would somehow change his life.

FOUND | 1

NAVIN HELD A journal in his right, gloved hand. He had found it, just lying there, on a Manhattan street. It could have been anyone's journal, he thought, but it wasn't. It belonged to Steve Martin—the comedian, the actor, the author.

That Steve Martin.

Navin knew it was Steve Martin's journal by what was written within. The journal's contents were, for any Steve Martin fan, unmistakable in their origins. Navin was most certainly a fan.

He flipped through and found silly setups and orphaned punch lines, as well as notes on art and intelligent prose. He intuitively navigated a rumbling city sidewalk held captive by the clutches of winter. But his skimming of the journal as he walked revealed references to movies, books and plays that leapt from its pages to enthrall him and often caused him to slow his pace or blindly brush an oncoming pedestrian.

Scribbles about "Rob," "Johnny" and "Jan" ignited Navin's imagination. He assumed these may have been references to "Reiner" and "Carson," but struggled for whom the scrawled "Jan" referred. "Hooks" and "-Michael Vincent" were possible surnames for "Jan." But he thought the former was a stretch and the latter made no sense whatsoever.

Written reminders to contact "Marty's agent" or "Lorne's assistant" placed, in Navin's way of thinking, great value upon the book. Surely, Navin thought, Steve Martin will want—check that, *need*—this journal returned to him.

If most of these clues failed to confirm the journal was Steve Martin's, the hint on the second page of the book spelled it out in graceful cursive:

Steve Martin's journal:
The comedian, the actor, the author

So, indeed, this journal held the thoughts of Steve Martin. *That* Steve Martin.

By improbable coincidence, the finder of Steve Martin's journal was Navin R. Johnson. That Navin's first job was as a gas station attendant in a St. Louis, Missouri suburb exceeded all embodiment of irony. But, that he had also once guessed peoples' weight for a carnival was, well, simply improbable.

But it was true: A former carnie and gas station attendant named Navin R. Johnson found Steve Martin's journal on the sidewalk outside the Lexington Avenue entrance of the Waldorf Astoria Hotel in New York City, in the painful cold of a January day.

While distracted by the journal's pages, he mindlessly made a series of right-hand turns and returned to the spot where he had rescued the journal from a certain trampling by pedestrians. He paused for a moment, looked around, and gave a calculating stare to the revolving door of the landmark's lesser-known portal. He timed an opening and stepped in and through the door.

Still enamored with his find, he continued to flip through the journal as he rode the escalator that carried him to ornate shop windows and past famed restaurants.

The corridors opened into a cube-shaped room. In a

lounge to his right, well-attired people were getting a very early jump on happy hour. A clock rose dead ahead to mark the lobby's center and the time of day. Just off his left shoulder, three men in uniform huddled around something of interest at the concierge desk, as if it were summer and the New York Yankees were on television.

Beyond the concierge, to his far left, extended the lengthy counter recessed into a wall-long niche. Shaking from the cold and slapping his gloved hands, he approached the front desk where Tiffany greeted him with a smile.

"I have Steve Martin's journal," Navin said. "I'd like to return it to him, please."

Tiffany gawked at Navin blankly who, despite being indoors, was as wrapped in his winter outer garments as tightly as a burrito. All she could see of him were his eyes, which shot from between the top of a black scarf and the bottom of a black tuque. Tiffany recognized nearly too late that her silent processing of Navin's claim (and rather terrorist-esque wardrobe) was causing an awkward pregnant pause. She took a deep breath and rushed a remedy by squinting at him and saying, "Oh, the actor Steve Martin?"

"Yeah," Navin said. "Steve Martin. Comedian and

author, too. I found it in the street." He pointed to no place in particular. "Outside. In the, uh, street."

"Oh, of course," she said. She pecked the keyboard a few times and clicked the computer's mouse, then greeted his eyes with hers once more. "I don't see Steve Martin as a guest, either currently or recently checked out."

Navin pulled the scarf with his gloved hand to uncover his nose and mouth, which caused Tiffany to grin. "Oh," he said. "Well, you know, he probably wouldn't check in under his real name, would he?"

"Oh, I don't know, sir."

"Don't they usually check in under fake names?"

"Celebrities?"

"Yeah."

"We do have some guests who like to be anonymous. I'll be right back. A moment, please?"

"Of course."

Tiffany, as identified by her gold-plated nametag, reached below the counter and pulled a tethered handset. She turned her back to Navin so, he presumed, she would not be overheard. Navin appreciated Tiffany's discretion.

She wore a navy-blue business jacket over a crisp, white shirt. Her navy-blue skirt fell just below her knees. Her black hair was pulled tightly and formed a ponytail that fell to just below the height of her shoulders. She was a uniformed member of the reception desk's army. But he noted she displayed an attractive ease, and this ease illuminated her more brightly than the rest—like a neon vacancy sign on a dark and tired highway. Perhaps, he thought, this is why he went to her.

Navin, with no place he needed to be, held the journal with both hands waist high and was giddy to do so. His eyes scanned up and along the desk before returning to gaze at the back of Tiffany's head. Even her ponytail, he thought, shone brightly. His mind drifted until he sparkled upon the thought that Steve Martin may be in the cavernous lobby at any moment, and he could then return the journal personally.

A chance meeting with Steve Martin would be tidy and efficient. In this way, Navin thought, the journal would never leave his careful guard. He turned and scoped the lobby for Steve Martin with an outward calm that betrayed the dither within. "Certainly he needs this returned," he said beneath his breath.

Navin would never admit he was one for celebrity sightings. Typically brushes with fame didn't excite him.

They only made him curious. But he was a Steve Martin fan. Once, over cocktails with friends, Steve Martin appeared on his list of the top five people, living or dead, with whom he would like to have dinner. Sir Winston Churchill, Pablo Picasso, Peter O'Toole and Lee Harvey Oswald completed the list.

Tiffany startled Navin with a stern, "Sir?"

"Oh, uh, yes?" he said turning to face her.

"Steve Martin is not a guest here, and we are very sure he's not registered under an alias."

Navin paused. "Oh," he said. "Well . . . thanks." He turned away only to quickly turn back. He paused again, looked to the journal and extended it toward Tiffany. "Well, what do I do with this now?"

She thought. "Turn it into a screenplay?" she asked, then she smiled and said, "Good day." And with that, her eyes sparkled once more and she turned away.

Navin nodded, turned back and began his walk through the richness and scale of the Waldorf's gut and down the escalators that led to the revolving doors that fanned Lexington Avenue's sidewalk. Stinging cold awaited him.

He fired from the Waldorf's revolving doors and a doorman, his hands pocketed as if his wrists were handcuffed beneath his parka, wished him a good afternoon. This lone and bundled doorman stood outside with seemingly nothing to do. There were no taxi doors to open or luggage to carry. Navin did not recall ever seeing a doorman on this side of the hotel. But, just the same, the doorman's salutation did nothing to snap Navin from his preoccupation with Steve Martin's journal. And so, ignoring the doorman's adieu, Navin asked, "Have you seen Steve Martin today?"

"No, sir, I have not," the doorman said, his words filling the space before him in the form of a cloud.

"Ummm, well, look: I found his journal right over there, so I think he's been around. If you see Steve Martin, could you let him know I have his journal and give him my card?" Navin pulled a business card and a pen from his inside coat pocket and turned the card over to its unprinted side. He began to write. "I'm staying at the Marriott up there until Wednesday," he said as he pointed down Lexington Avenue and across 49th Street. "It'll be there until then. I put my mobile number on the card . . . there," he said, pointing with the tip of his pen.

"If I see Steve Martin I will give this to him," the doorman said. "We are talking about *the* Steve Martin, the actor?"

"Of course!" Navin said. "Comedian and author, also. And actor. Of course."

"Of course," the doorman said. He pulled a hand from his pocket, took the card and returned his hand to its den. "All that."

Navin looked to his left at the oncoming one-way traffic, sprinted across the street to the opposite sidewalk and turned south toward New York's Marriott East Side. He stomped the slush and snow from his boots and entered the hotel, moved directly ahead to the elevator bank, and jostled his way into the path of closing elevator doors.

The doors squeezed him then reluctantly sprung open, allowing him to enter the small, antique elevator car. He removed his scarf and then his cap from his head. His full, blond hair settled without order.

An elderly woman's feigned smile revealed her impatience for Navin, though he missed its meaning. He returned a smile which caused the dimple on his left cheek to deepen. His eyes, as blue as light, were coated by tears from the cold wind outdoors. He pressed them closed and cleared his vision, sending a drop down his cheek. The journal pulled his freshly corrected sight downward.

His inspection of the book grew acute as the elevator gently rocked its occupants to the higher floors. Its sound was reminiscent of the softened clanking of a passenger train from a classic Hollywood film.

Time lapsed and Navin found himself alone in the elevator car. His attention to Steve Martin's journal caused him to miss the elderly woman's exit. He also failed to notice that he had taken two round trips, up and down, during which the elevator car made twelve stops and carried eighteen passengers. Navin snapped back to the present, removed his right hand from the journal and poked the 6 button. The car began to ascend once again and delivered him to his floor.

He took a right turn and noticed he was wading in the earthy aroma of aged wood and, when he closed his eyes, this essence reminded him of his grandmother's house.

Navin's room was a corner unit whose north view overlooked 49th Street. Through these windows, he could see the intersection of 49th and Lexington Avenue down and to the left. Diagonally through the intersection he had a crow's-nest view of the Lexington Avenue entrance to the Waldorf Astoria, and its lone doorman, who still had nothing to do and remained alone in the cold.

An architectural recess on the north side of the building gave him a view to the east. From here, his view of the relatively tiny Smith & Wollensky's green-and-white façade nearly a full block away beckoned him conspicuously from the corner of Third Avenue and 49th Street. He returned the stare, and in passing thought steak and a stiff drink sounded delicious. He closed his eyes and turned and placed Steve Martin's journal on the console that held a flat-screen television. He tossed his hat and scarf onto the floor next to a green armchair that sat in the corner between the two sets of windows. He cast his coat onto the chair, lofted his sweater toward his suitcase on the floor, and kicked his boots in no intended direction.

He stood dressed only in a pair of tight, white long underpants and an equally tight, matching long-sleeved shirt. He ran his hands through his receding hairline, an inevitability of age that suited him. His eyebrows were a shade of blond darker than the hair on his head. They arced up toward the bridge of his nose, which ski-sloped to a soft point. His eyes, clear now of the tears, were big and round and sparkled with the echo of the sconces that hung on the wall. His eyes were inviting and, despite their fatigue, they suggested an age younger than his forty-four years. His lips were full, and a slight gap between his top two front teeth provided the endearing character of an imperfect smile. His sideburns were, like his eyebrows, a darker variety of blond. They were trimmed and squared at the bottom. They fell to just above the bottom of his ear lobes, framed his face and guarded his ears. The suggestion of his dimple remained even on an expressionless face. Navin's life in South Florida kept him well-tanned, though much of his color had been muted by the harsh New York freeze and his lightly hued whiskers. But, despite this seamless combination and arrangement of features, something in his eyes suggested his allure was fragile and conditional.

    His underwear clung to him and revealed a former athlete's body. There was some tone in his forearms, calves and chest. A decade and a half of a sedentary lifestyle, however, had caused some fat to insulate his six-foot-tall frame. His nails were crisply manicured. His eyebrows were devoid of unruly and ambitious hair follicles, as were his nostrils and ears. He tended to the more unsightly details of his appearance, but the rest he left to simply be.

    His eyes fell upon Steve Martin's journal that rested

next to the television, and then around the room. He peered to the window that overlooked Lexington Avenue. He turned his head back to the journal and rubbed his eyes with the palms of his hands. An eventful day had caught him.

"I need a nap," he said aloud to no one, breaking the silence he had held since he had spoken to a lone doorman.

☙

Steve Martin walked into the Marriott East Side hotel, made a sharp right and marched to the reception desk. He was instantly recognized by nearly all within the Marriott lobby. He appeared as the public knew him: dressed in a sharp blazer and tie beneath a winter coat of propriety, his white hair combed neatly and his face cleanly shaven. He wore black-rimmed eyeglasses on this day, though they hardly served as a disguise. If he had noticed the few who pointed, whispered and snapped pictures of him with their camera phones, he failed to let on. Like a stone thrown into a placid pond, his arrival anywhere caused disruption to routines and order. But this was Manhattan, and New Yorkers are the world's second best (behind only the French) at being unimpressed. And so boats rocked from his wake, and their passengers acted as if they were effortlessly tilting their glasses to prevent their drinks from spilling.

And it was because of this that he was left to himself and able to use the time, a benefit of being second in line, to notice the two pieces of art that hung to the right of the hotel's reception desk. His eyes moved through the paintings. He identified how particular artistic effects were created. The work's luminosity caught his scrutiny. The artist's technique struck him as familiar.

"Checking in, Mr. Martin?" a man's voice asked from behind the reception desk.

"Uh, no, actually," Steve said as his head turned toward the voice but his eyes remained fixed on the art. "Look, this is going to sound a little silly, but I am looking for a Navin R. Johnson. I believe he is a guest here."

Expecting Steve to be funny, the receptionist exploded with laughter. "That's a good one!" he said. "Have you checked the phonebook over there? They're new, and I hear he *is* somebody now."

Steve recognized the reference to his film The Jerk, as he had countless times before. "Yes, aha," he said as his head tipped back and forward again. "That's very quick. A fan. Thank you. But seriously, I believe he is a guest here. Here's his card, could you check please?"

After a quick scan of the computer monitor in front of him, the receptionist said, "Uh, yes, actually he is a guest," and returned the card to Steve. "May I call and announce that you are here to see him?"

"No, I can just use a courtesy phone."

"Won't take a moment . . ."

"Well, yes then, please. Thanks."

"My pleasure." The receptionist dialed Navin's room.

Steve scoped the hotel lobby, careful to not make eye contact with anyone. After a second pass, Steve looked down to Navin's business card:

Thoughts, Inc.
Navin R. Johnson

The reverse of the card was smeared with blotches of water soluble ink caused by the wet winter elements. Navin's scribbles had melted, but were still readable. Steve sensed there was no answer in Navin's room. Then confirmation.

"Mr. Martin, I'm afraid there is no answer," said the

receptionist. "Shall I leave a message?"

"Does this hotel have a voicemail system?"

"Yes, it does."

"I'll call in and leave one myself," Steve said. He left the hotel and jaunted across the street and up the block to the Waldorf.

"Any luck, Mr. Martin?" the lone Waldorf doorman asked without removing his hands from their refuge.

"Uh, no," Steve said graciously and smiled. "Thanks." He slid between two moving fins of the revolving door and was sucked into the building.

In a window shade-darkened Room 612 at the Marriott, a telephone ring startled Navin from sleep. He responded to the second ring by covering his head with a pillow. The third prompted him to rise quickly from the waist like the loaded arm of a catapult.

His dream had just foretold that Steve Martin was calling to claim his journal. He cleared his throat, picked up the phone and placed it to his ear.

"Hello?" he said.

"Mr. Johnson, thesis howskeepeeng," a voice in broken English said. "We see you had a 'Doo Not Deesturbs' on your door, and won to know if you need clean towels."

Navin paused to cross the line between dream and reality.

"Sir?" the housekeeping department representative asked.

"Um," he said, and cleared his voice again. "No, thank you. I have all I need." He blinked. "Thank you."

ॐ

It was early evening now and Navin had fallen back asleep to continue his nap, and unwittingly rejoin his dream of Steve Martin's quest to retrieve his journal. This time as Navin slept, he was very aware that he was, in fact, dreaming. His thoughts about what he saw served as a running commentary.

Navin the Sleeper watched as the protagonist of this dream—himself—left the Marriott to return to the Waldorf. Navin the Sleeper was aware that Navin the Protagonist was unaware that he trailed Steve by just moments, but there was nothing Navin the Sleeper could do to help. Navin the Protagonist reached the revolving doors, where he was stopped by the doorman.

"You've just missed him," the doorman said as he freed one hand to gesture to the door.

"Steve Martin?" Navin asked.

"Yes," the doorman said.

"No!" yelled Navin the Sleeper in his silent observation. "Steve the Roto-Rooter guy from Chattanooga!"

"I gave him your card and he went to the Marriott to find you," the doorman said.

"Steve Martin?" Navin asked.

Navin the Sleeper felt his eyes roll beneath closed lids.

Without thanking the doorman, Navin turned and burst through the revolving doors, then climbed the escalator steps. Certain he would know Steve when he saw him, he carefully looked into each shop and restaurant that led to the Waldorf's front desk.

"Slow down," thought Navin the Sleeper. "You'll miss him."

At the Waldorf's front desk Navin, panting, returned to Tiffany, glowing. "He's here," Navin said. "Can you please look once more?"

Her light was extinguished by her misreading his excitement as something more nefarious, and it failed to register with him that he had alarmed her.

"You must look once more," Navin insisted. "I have his journal."

"You're . . . I'm . . . we're scaring her . . .," Navin the Sleeper warned.

"Steve Martin?" she asked.

"No!" he snapped. "Steve the Roto-Rooter guy from Chattanooga."

"Sir," she said with growing unease, "Steve Martin is not registered as a guest in this hotel. I'm sorry, but he is not."

Across the Waldorf lobby, Steve broke stride slightly when an intimidating doorman, en route with mild urgency to Navin and Tiffany, cut across his path. Having evaded a collision, Steve continued his trek toward an attractive woman in her early sixties.

"Oh my god," Navin the Sleeper thought.

This magnetic lady—with sparkling silver hair complemented by ornate-yet-tasteful black onyx earrings, a long red-leather coat and matching hat—looked as if she had inspired the phrase "salt of the earth." Steve recognized a mumbled commotion to his left, but was not compelled to look. He had learned to tune out unrest around him, as much of it was caused by his very presence.

"Can I speak with a manager?" Navin pleaded at the desk. "I think Mr. Martin really needs to have this returned to him."

"Sir, he will tell you the same—there is no Steve Martin registered," Tiffany insisted.

"A manager, please," he countered.

"Can I help?" a stern voice said from behind Navin's left ear.

"Yes," Navin said as he turned his body to the voice. "I need to see a manager."

Across the lobby, the woman spotted Steve as he approached her and broke into a warming smile. She rose from her chair to greet him with a hug.

"Did you find it?" she asked.

"No answer in his room," Steve said.

"What now?" she asked.

"I'll call over and leave a message on his voicemail," he said.

The manager gave Tiffany a reassuring look and said, "Sir, I am the manager, and Steve Martin is not staying at the Waldorf, and now I really must insist that we show you the way out."

"But—" Navin began.

"You have Steve Martin's journal," the manager finished acerbically.

"Let's go back up to your room and I'll call over to the Marriott," Steve suggested to the woman.

"Really, sir, you must go now," the manager urged Navin as his eyes began to wander, perhaps in search of some larger assistance.

"If you go ahead, Steve, I'll bring us some coffee up," the woman said.

"There is nothing you can do to help?" Navin asked the manager.

"He's behind you!" thought Navin the Sleeper. "Steve Martin is behind you."

"Cream?" the woman asked Steve.

"No, I don't think I would like any coffee," Steve said.

A pit formed in Navin the Sleeper's stomach. "Why is *she* here?"

"We've done all we can, and all we're willing to do, sir," the manager said to Navin.

Steve and the woman turned to their left to head in the direction of the elevators. Dejected and with fallen eyes, Navin turned to his right to leave. Navin took a few inattentive steps and collided with Steve's lady friend.

For a moment the lady and Navin locked eyes. He was crippled by shock. She appeared to be as stunned as well. In a moment, Navin's eyes grew submissive, content. She was radiant.

"Mom?" Navin asked.

"Mom," Navin the Sleeper thought.

"Navin! Darling!" Mom said.

"Why are you in New York?" Navin asked.

"You knew Steve and I were here for his banjo tour, honey. You know, you should also read his autobiography. A really clever title."

"How would I know that?" Navin the Sleeper asked.

"Steve?" a confused Navin asked, not knowing to whom she was referring. His disorientation had stalled him.

The ambient buzz in the lobby grew silent. A muffled symphony of taxi cab horns on Park Avenue died abruptly and brought peace to the streets of Midtown. All things had stopped moving. A tossed Styrofoam coffee cup hung above a trash bin as chestnut colored droplets hovered in mid-spin from the cup's radius. Airplanes hung in the sky, as did a suicide jumper in Harlem.

Tiffany's head was thrust back in suspended laughter in response to some unknown wit. The manager was motionless with his upper teeth pressed against his lower lip in mid-speech. "He must have been making a 'vee' or an 'eff' sound," Navin the Sleeper thought. And Lee Harvey Oswald was in mid-stride, having just entered the lobby from the elevator bank.

"Of course, darling, *Steve*," Mom said.

"I don't know *Steve*," Navin said, mocking his mother's emphasis.

"Of course you do, dear—the comedian? The actor? The author?" Mom explained.

"I didn't know you had any children, Bry," Steve said to the woman.

"Of course you did, Steve," Bry said.

"No, I really didn't," Steve said.

Bry tilted her head to the right and smiled, prompting Steve to return her warmth. Bry could make anyone stop and smile, in any circumstance, by simply tilting her head.

Steve extended his hand and introduced himself to Navin. "Steve Martin," he said.

"I'm Navin R. Johnson," Navin said.

"If you knew how many times I got that from people," Steve said with forced graciousness. "You know what else I get? Neal Page. And sometimes really *jolly* guys come up and identify themselves as the 'shower curtain-ring guy.'"

"Uh, no, really," Navin said in a trancelike tone. "My name is Navin R. Johnson." Navin sought to find the words to tell Steve that he had his journal. But the thought that, by all appearances, his mother was Steve's lover upset and confused him. There was silence and he found nothing to say. "I was once a carnie," he said.

Steve laughed again. "At least it's not like it used to be," Steve said, still convinced Navin was joking. "It did not even take *ten* walks through airports for me to live to regret that whole 'wild-and-crazy-guy' thing."

"Um, no," Navin said. "My name *really is* Navin."

Steve's smile vanished. It appeared he had remembered something. He pulled a business card from his pocket.

Steve looked in each direction to discover Tiffany laughing in perpetuity, and Lee Harvey Oswald frozen in the lobby of the Waldorf.

"Walk over here with me," Steve said to Navin. He turned to Bry and gave a comforting nod.

"Mom never liked Steve Martin," Navin the Sleeper thought.

Steve lead Navin into the shadow cast by a grand staircase and, once he was sure none of the immobile living that now occupied the Waldorf's lobby were within earshot, looked Navin squarely in the eyes with a deciphering squint.

"Yes?" asked Navin.

Steve's squint intensified.

"Well?" asked Navin.

Steve cased the lobby of stiffs once more until his eyes met with Bry's. He raised a hand with a two-finger wave, and Bry smiled and tilted her head. Steve dropped his shoulders and smiled widely. His attention, and a resurging squint, snapped to Navin.

"Why are you screwing with me?" Steve mumbled.

"Uh, I'm sor–," Navin squeaked.

"Why are you trying to screw with me, Navin?" Steve Martin was uncharacteristically mean.

"I don't, uh, I have your—"

"Is it because I'm having sex your mom? You don't think your mom has ever had sex before? How the hell do you think *you* got here? You're not Jesus, you know?"

"Jesus?"

"Jesus," an impatient Steve Martin said through gritted teeth. "*Jesus*! Freaking *JESUS*. You didn't know he was an immaculate—?"

"No, yeah, I—"

"Immaculate conception." Steve stepped back to gather his thoughts. He drew a deep breath that flared his nostrils.

"That's the same look he had when he had discovered Del Griffith had stolen his credit card," Navin the Sleeper thought.

"Can I help out, Steve?" Lee Harvey Oswald said after approaching Steve from behind.

"I have to wake up," Navin the Sleeper thought.

"Shoot this gravy-sucking . . .," Steve said as his voice trailed away.

"What?" Navin asked.

"And don't get caught this time," Steve said.

Lee, who both Navins thought looked pretty fit for an allegedly old and reportedly dead guy, pulled a gun from his gray wool coat and placed the barrel beneath Navin's chin. He pressed the cold steel to Navin's skin and pushed his nose to the ceiling.

"Please, I just wanted . . .," Navin pleaded with clenched teeth. Tears suddenly formed in the corners of his eyes.

"I really have to wake up," Navin the Sleeper thought. This time, he sensed he had said it aloud in his sleep.

Lee pulled the trigger but the only noise the gun made was the ding-dong of a doorbell.

"Mom?" Navin whimpered.

"C'mon!" Steve yelled.

Again, Lee pulled the trigger.

Ding-dong.

"Shoot him!" Steve yelled.

Ding-dong.

"Oh, for . . .," Steve said. "Jack was right. You're incompetent."

Lee dropped his hands and sagged his shoulders as if his feelings had been hurt, freeing Navin's head to drop. Navin turned his tear-filled eyes toward Bry. "Mom?"

"Give me that goddamn thing!" Steve said while ripping the pistol from Lee's hand.

Bry looked at Navin and gave a mother-knows-best smile, lovingly tilted her head to one side and shrugged her shoulders. Navin broke into a content smile.

"Why didn't you let me watch Steve Martin when I was younger," Navin the Sleeper asked. "Just because you didn't like him?"

Ding-dong.

"MOM!" Navin shouted. He turned back toward Lee and Steve. Steve stood above Lee's body—a body whose life was draining onto the spotless floor of the Waldorf Astoria. Steve's posture was as bold as a victorious matador. He looked down at his kill without emotion. The gun dangled from his right hand, which hung at Steve's side. Lee gasped a breath and his eyes crossed slightly. And then he exhaled. Lee had been shot dead for the second time in a half-century.

"Christ, Steve!" Navin said.

Steve slowly squared around to Navin, squinted one last time, raised the pistol to Navin's forehead, and pulled the trigger.

"Oh, god," Navin—and Navin the Sleeper—said together.

FROZEN | 2

DING-DONG.

Navin's entire body twitched in the disorienting darkness. "What . . .," Navin began.

Ding-dong.

He jumped again.

"Steve is a very funny and talented man." Bry's voice reverberated within his head. "Navin, I'd love you if you were the color of a baboon's ass."

"*What?*" Navin said aloud.

Ding-dong.

Navin opened his eyes. Though confused and disoriented, he noted that the light through the window had turned a deep blue and washed Marriott Guest Room 612 in a hue of calming and robust purple. The room's only other light source came from his ringing cell phone.

Ding-dong.

Still lying on his back, he grabbed the phone, held it above his eyes and struggled to read the display. He had no interest as to who was calling. In fact, that it was a phone call failed to register at all. He most likely looked to the screen by some instinctual mechanism to establish his bearings. In one moment he was about to be shot dead by Steve Martin, and in the next he was rescued by his phone's doorbell ringtone. Fresh from escaping his own murder and slightly cognizant that he was receiving a phone call, he remained groggy and stunned, as well as inept to answer the phone. He rubbed his eyes, groaned and tossed it to the table.

He moved his hand to his chest to feel his pounding heart. He recognized the startling sensation that lingered after an afternoon nap had carried into dusk. He was confused. He was unsure if it was still Monday, or if he had slept straight through to Tuesday's dawn. "Am I late for something?" he thought.

He sought the time from the digital clock next to the bed to discover it was 8:14. It was too dark, Navin reasoned, for it to be 8:14 in the morning. It had to be Monday night. It was his second-to-last night in New York.

Navin began to orientate himself, but remnants of

his dream left him feeling uneasy. Moments later, he realized his anxiety was caused by something personal, perhaps about someone who had been loitering in his brain for a while.

He wondered who it could be. Forgiving Steve Martin was easy. "He is a very funny and talented man," he thought. But while Steve was a very funny and talented man, Lee Harvey Oswald was not. And if he were funny, it had not been documented. He was just a peculiar protagonist of controversy, conspiracy and confusion. Navin was certain that despite this dream, the original opinions he held for each remained unaltered.

He hardly knew Tiffany, though he had a very strong sense that he liked her. In a rare and fleeting moment of bold optimism he considered visiting her tomorrow to ask her out. He was, he reasoned, empowered by being a visitor in New York after all.

He thought about his mother. An idea darted through his mind and caused a physical cringe and an audible, shameful groan. But the thought went as quickly as it came, and left him to sit tensely and attempt hopelessly to recapture that notion so that a revelation could follow. His mother, he thought, must be the cause of the angst with which he awoke.

While Oswald's unorthodox cameo in the dream may have overshadowed many of the important details Navin required to make sense of it all, a number of questions overwhelmed Navin—queries that would simmer in his head and test the competence of his subconscious logic for much of the remaining evening.

"Why on Earth would I dream that my mom was dating Steve Martin?" he asked himself. His mother did not like Steve Martin's comedy or movies. Whenever he appeared on television, she would often scoff, "Oh, it's *that* guy." She grew particularly irritated when she would tune in to see her favorite, Johnny Carson, only to find that, "*That* guy has hijacked my program." It occurred to him that Steve Martin had redefined her son's wonderful name for his first film, and that his mother may have held a grudge.

Navin's internal dialogue flowed. "Why was Steve Martin dating my mom? Why would he be so crass about it? Why would he think I was up to something? Was he going to hurt my mom? Why would I be so adamant to return a journal as to nearly be physically removed from a landmark hotel? How could my mom's boyfriend and I not know of each other's existence? And why would she insist otherwise?

"Why did Steve Martin keep calling my mom 'Bry'?" He paused for a moment, looked back to his phone and rubbed his eyes with the palms of his hands again. "Her name is Doris," he said aloud.

Questions like these fluttered about Navin's brain like moths around a porch light. As they ricocheted in his skull, he rolled himself from his bed and walked to the bathroom. He stared himself down in the mirror above the sink, then unscrewed the cap from a worn and dented tube of toothpaste. He applied a bead to a toothbrush that had outlived its effectiveness and brushed his teeth.

He turned on the shower and allowed the water to warm. He stepped timidly into the tub and stood beneath the water for a moment before washing. Once he began, he made quick work of the process. He rinsed and turned off the water. The air in his room was cold, so he toweled so quickly he nearly gave his shoulders and back friction burns. He dressed for dinner.

The questions taunted Navin as he left his room for the curb to hire a taxi. This dream had an unyielding grip on his consciousness. "Why," he eventually asked himself, "is this dream still on my mind?"

The Marriott's doorman whistled a taxi for Navin, and one pulled forward. The cab door was opened, and he simply stepped inside while graciously tipping the doorman five dollars in crinkly singles. Navin announced his destination to the driver, and the car pulled from the crushed ice and snow that had gathered throughout the day in the gutters along Lexington Avenue.

⊂℟

Navin finished a hearty meal of pasta and veal at Celeste on the island's Upper West Side, and left the restaurant to flag down the taxi that would return him to the Marriott. It had grown much colder now. He did not have the assistance of a doorman, a whistle, or the efficient combination of the two. Nonetheless, he had good fortune in that a taxi was his within moments.

Years of unchecked service on New York City's streets had converted the taxi into a rolling trampoline. The vehicle bounded, bouncing Navin about each time it met a cross street—a dip, a quick mound and a second quick dip. As his head missed hitting the taxi's ceiling by an inch, his eyes remained fixed upon the sights. Staunchly lit storefronts and isolated frozen pedestrians waiting at crosswalks whizzed by him. The car surfed the waves of the city's intersections, and Navin's thoughts landed on the journal, the dream and what these things meant.

"Maybe I just don't have anything else to think about," Navin thought. "I need a pastime."

New York life continued to roll by effortlessly until the Waldorf Astoria appeared to the right side of the car and snapped him from a lost stare. A moment later, he arrived at the Marriott. "Eight dollars," the taxi driver said with a dense accent.

Navin pulled three loose balls of crumpled paper money from each pocket and sorted through them until he found a ten-dollar bill. He negotiated the cash until he found another bill and handed the driver eleven dollars. "Keep it," Navin said.

"Thanks you," the driver said.

"Be safe." He slid out of the taxi's left-rear door.

The taxi's weight crushed the ice as it pulled away, and the sound this made was a detail that caught Navin's attention. He stood and faced the front of the hotel. A look at his watch revealed it was ten of 11, but Navin was fresh from a nap, shower and dinner and really didn't feel like surrendering to the confines of a generic hotel room. Besides, he would be leaving for his home in Florida the day after next. Once home, there would be no sound of weighted rubber on crunching ice. He had not yet had enough of the city.

To brave the cold, he pulled the scarf from around his neck to cover his mouth and nose, and turned north to take a walk and, more specifically, find a cocktail.

The night was bitterly cold. But he loved visiting the city, and reasoned a very cold walk in Manhattan was better than a very warm bed in his South Florida home. Further, any drink in the hotel bar is not adventurous. He always felt as though he might miss something uniquely local if he hung out with travelers.

At first the walk seemed manageable, and at first it was. The weather conditions only stung when the buildings that lined Lexington Avenue vanished at intersections and allowed the assaulting eastbound crosswinds to shred through Navin's body. He was invigorated. He was out of his room, in the city, and feeling like a New Yorker if for no other reason than he was in New York. "Hey," Navin thought, "if I lived here, this is what I would be doing."

As he walked, his thoughts finally returned to the honor he had been given earlier in the day. "Pioneer Award," he mumbled beneath his scarf. "I don't know what that means." Soon, his mind assumed the character that was his public persona. He began to replay and edit his acceptance speech in his mind. He identified what would have been most entertaining, most compelling.

He critiqued his performance. He not only had a knack for message, but its delivery as well. So, such personal debriefs were not uncommon for Navin and because of them he was a very effective speaker.

As he walked, he shamelessly enjoyed the remembrance of the laughs he drew, but laughs that he did not recognize as he spoke. This often happened when he was "on." His concentration on his presentation caused him to ignore reaction. Reaction was seemingly dropped into a depository for later review. When he was ready, he could easily reunite his performance with the reaction it drew.

Soon, his active imagination took his alter ego to an imaginary television interview and then a game show that he created as he walked. It was a game he played. The nature of the exercise was automatic, and though he didn't know why or when it would happen, he assumed it was a subconscious writing exercise.

But three artic blasts and just two blocks later, Navin's practice was refuted by a sudden and mumbled, "What the fuck am I doing?" beneath his scarf. "I'm not a New

Yorker, and it's minus one hundred. I think it's worth trekking through this shit to get a bit of New York in me?"

He had identified a problem, but if he was anything, he was stubborn. "First bar," he thought, "I'm going in. But I'm not turning back." Unfortunately, if he passed any establishments that would serve him a cocktail, he didn't notice. He walked with purpose. His head was down and he muttered to himself along the way. As he approached the rare passerby, he would reduce the volume of his voice as to not be heard.

This audible conversation, however, was not an exercise. It was a mechanism, a device to serve as distraction from the arctic blast with which he was dealing. It quickly, however, evolved into a bitch session about the very topic from which he was trying to be distracted.

"Why the hell does the weather have to be this goddamn extreme when I come here?" Navin complained to whoever controlled the weather. "And why the fuck do I decide to get out in it?"

Slowly, his stream of consciousness led him toward a destination as uncharted as that of the walk itself.

"I take a nap so late that I have to eat late and then I'm not ready for bed," he thought. "I go to dinner and the cab ride costs nearly as much as the meal. I pay eleven dollars to get to an eighteen-dollar dinner. It's a thirty-dollar meal. I could have gotten a Waldorf salad for less than thirty dollars. And I could have gotten it at the fucking Waldorf.

"And that's if they would have let me in after that whole blow up at the desk with Tiffany and Steve Martin and Lee Harvey Oswald. Who has dreams like these? When did Steve become pals with Lee Harvey Oswald? When did he start dating Doris?

"I bet if I turn back now, I can find pages and pages in Steve Martin's journal that uncloak the whole JFK thing. And why did I have to find that thing anyway? To anyone else, it's an eBay auction item. To me, it's something else. Dreams. I have this journal for ninety minutes, and Steve Martin is poking my mom in my dreams. And do I think I'll meet Steve Martin and he'll thank me and we'll become buddies? Why is this such a big deal?"

Suddenly, Navin's reality commanded his attention. His stream of consciousness stopped cold. He stopped walking. He felt the sudden twinge of panic an ocean swimmer must feel when they have lost sight of land. "Where am I?" he asked. He looked ahead, and turned to look back. Lexington Avenue disappeared in the winter fog in both directions, seemingly endless. The Marriott was no longer within view. Nothing, in fact, was.

Suddenly, he realized that his thighs were burning and his ears were stinging. His runny nose had become such a physical source of frustration that fighting the urge to rip off his scarf and gloves to barbarically claw at it became a test of his willpower.

Prudence prevailed, and he quickly turned and began walking back toward the Marriott. The wind blew in his face now. He had forgotten his rant of moments before. His only thoughts were of the bitter cold, that his toes felt like stones, and that he should stop in the first bar or pub he passed to warm up and have a drink. An Irish coffee sounded like a perfect remedy and, besides, a nonstop return walk would be beyond miserable, if not certain death.

As Navin crossed the intersecting numbered streets, he looked in each direction for a tavern or bar that might be just off Lexington Avenue. 68th Street. 67th Street. 66th Street. Nothing.

"Jesus, where is the Marriott?" he stammered. "52nd? 50th? I don't even know. Is it in the forties?"

He had no idea how far he had walked. His

conversation to 68th Street took him from his thirty-dollar salad, to the events of today, imagining he was on a television game show, and then to Steve Martin.

He came to the 59th Street subway station and walked to its top step. "There has to be a stop near the hotel," he thought. He wasn't sure. "Nine blocks? Ten? Less? I don't know."

His knack for indecision often temporarily paralyzed him. When this paralyses married his tendency to see every quest through no matter the ratio of pain to gain, the result was often a self-inflicted shot to his self-worth. He viewed himself as a good soldier. And he was. A fighter. And that he was, as well. One who doesn't quit. And he thought he never had.

But his inability to assess the risk and the rewards of his personal endeavors mostly led to inexplicable emptiness. He often only knew unmistakable failure from heroic efforts. It was as if he had run twenty-six miles but never found the marathon's finish line.

He never could pull himself far enough away to see that he was running very quickly to a location that held nothing for him. But worse, no one was there to redirect him. Or to run with him. Or to be grateful that he tried.

His faith often misled him. If he kept putting in, he

reasoned, he would get something out. But he never noticed the depository he fed often had no mechanism to dispense anything.

Navin looked down the stairwell of the 59th Street station as the wind sliced between his ribs. He danced in place from the cold. He looked up and down Lexington Avenue. "I came out to get a drink, and I am going to get a drink," he said. "I'm in New York."

If he ever passed a bar or a lounge on Lexington Avenue between 58th Street and 49th Street, he didn't see it. His walk became a living, physically painful metaphor for his perception of his very existence. The remainder of his journey hurt, and as the number of each street he crossed lowered by one so did his sense of self-worth. From 59th Street to the Marriott at 49th Street, he had devalued his ego ten points.

Through the fog, the bright-orange heat lamps that hung above the Marriott's entrance landmarked the end of his misery. With each step the lamps glowed more brightly, until soon he stood beneath them and basked appreciatively in the warmth. Though to him they felt like one hundred and twenty degrees, he reasoned that more useful heat awaited him beyond the revolving doors.

Once in the hotel, he stopped and shook off some

cold. He looked straight to the bank of elevators and then left to the bar. "I came out for a drink," he said aloud. "I'm getting a drink." And so, he turned left.

He guided his near-frozen body past two business women sitting at a table in the lounge. At the farthest end of the bar sat a grossly overweight gentleman in a sloppy business suit, and an overly long and undistinguished loosened striped tie. He sat on the barstool nearest the hotel lobby and farthest from the lone bar patron.

With the bartender away, he allowed the ambient heat to reach his skin: he removed his hat, scarf and gloves and placed them on the barstool to his right, and draped his jacket over the stool's back. He rubbed his hands together to create friction and covered his ears with his warmed palms.

He exchanged nods with the businessman six or seven barstools away, fearful that it might invite a conversation. His desire to socialize diminished significantly sometime after his arrival by taxi to the Marriott's front doors and sometime before his arrival by foot following a deep-freezing, forty-block stroll. To ensure such an inconvenient exchange of pleasantries with the stranger at the bar could be avoided, Navin pulled his phone from his pocket and pretended to read and respond to a text message.

The bartender's absence began to annoy him. He had essentially spent thirty dollars on a meal, and walked forty blocks in a killer's freeze only to belly up to a hotel bar. But still, certainly a twenty-dollar martini would make it all OK. He checked and saw the empty inbox of his email account, looked at his calendar for a list of Tuesday's reminders, and turned his back to the bar to scan the virtually empty lounge and hotel lobby.

"We're closed up," a woman's small voice said from behind him.

He turned to her and after a jolt of disenchantment said, "Oh, OK. Goodnight." With that, he surrendered.

"Goodnight, sir," she said without looking up from the bar she had just begun to wipe. He thought for a moment of just how innocent her words were, but how they had won an entire war against his quest.

He stood slowly, draped his coat over his right forearm and gathered his accessories with his left hand. He walked briskly to the elevator and made his way to Room 612.

Once inside, he dropped his winter gear into the chair in the corner. He glanced out the north-facing windows to look at the classically lit, tiny structure that was Smith & Wollensky's. He sighed at the thought that their bar was probably open, and that it had been all day. He recalled the last time he was in town, he sat at that bar and listened to the bartender's thick Irish accent opine on world issues. "Damn, that would be perfect," he thought. But he had committed to his submission, and walking just one more block was simply out of the question.

He was warmer now, and he still wanted a drink. The in-room minibar offered an array of mini cocktail mixers and snacks. Over years of business travel, he had grown quite frivolous with hotel minibars. Toblerone. M&M's. Cashews and Coke. Pringles and Coke. Jack and Coke. Coke and Coke.

He opened the minibar and gave it a harsh study. He was to have but one drink and one snack, and he wanted to have no regrets. It had been, after all, an excruciating night. After toying with Oreo cookies and peanut brittle, he opted to forego the snack. He removed a mini Absolut Vodka and a soda water, took a glass from the counter, and took the items to his bed.

He mixed an iceless drink and drank it. He squirmed until he found comfort in lying on his back. He quietly thought how, just moments before at the hotel bar, he had finally given up on a painful-but-simple quest for a cocktail in any setting but in his room. This seemingly innocuous abdication was the latest in a series of tiny resignations in recent years. A sense of futility was swelling. He felt unrewarded in a life of effort, and so his indifference was displacing his spirit.

Beaten, he closed his eyes. "I tried," Navin said aloud. He drew a breath, sighed and opened his eyes to scan a dark ceiling. He closed his eyes again, said, "Damn it, Audrey," and fell asleep.

BEACHED | 3

"YOU DESERVE BETTER," Audrey said to Navin beneath a full moon on a South Florida beach. "I love you, but you deserve better."

"Yes, I do," Navin said. "And I deserve it from you."

"I can't give it," she said as tears began to fall from her eyes.

"Yes, you can," Navin said. "You choose not to. You are choosing to not enjoy what we have."

"No, Navin, I can't do that."

"Do what?"

"Be what you need," she said. She broke into a full sob. "And, yes, I choose not to."

Other than this, he thought it was a perfect night for romance. The breeze was light and titillating. The air cradled Audrey and Navin's skin. The sand beneath them carried the warmth of the day and absorbed their feet as gently as a down-filled bed. But there was no romance. She had chosen "not to."

He found himself surprisingly composed as he looked into a moonlit Atlantic Ocean and shook his head. "That doesn't make sense," he said above the whispered surf. "You are choosing to not follow your heart."

"I know," she said. "And I am choosing to not have a desire for you."

He felt her words chased a Daedalian logic, but he could not see beyond their detail. "What?" he asked. "Goddammit, Audrey, did you just mean to say for me, or did you mean in general?"

"For you," she said. She turned away from him and threw her arms to the sky. They quickly dropped and she added, "And in general. I generally don't want you."

He had never heard such a simple and strange sentence, or one so biting. "I generally don't want you?" he asked. "What does that mean? I don't know what that means."

"Don't make me tell you things you can't stand to hear," she said as she cried.

"Fucking decency calls for nothing less, Audrey. You can't get off this easily."

Her pause told him she was searching her vocabulary to carefully construct her next thought. Her brown eyes were shaped by dread. She sealed them shut for a moment, opened them and looked to the sea, then down to the sand. She raised her head and the wind pushed her shoulder-length black hair from her face. Her white wrap blew in the breeze and clung to her legs. Her olive skin grew goose pimples from the breeze. The wind gusted. Navin braced himself for a stinging message that would be masked, he predicted, by an inept effort to soften a blow. He waited, and waited some more, all the while thinking how beautiful he thought she was and how there was nothing she could say that she couldn't take back in time, or that he couldn't forgive, or that they couldn't discuss.

"You won't make enough money," she blurted.

Navin was stunned. He was stunned in that she actually verbalized this. But he was not surprised by her position on his finances. She had questioned his monetary ambition just months before, and so this wasn't new. He thought at the time that the disclosure of his worthwhile six-figure income had stilled her concerns. Though he thought he had calmed her, the remnants of that conversation had ever so slightly, nearly invisibly, colored his opinion of her. He was reluctantly aware that he filtered every action, every reaction and every interaction they shared against a fear that her affinity for him was borne more from the acquisition of lifestyle over the addiction of love.

It was a choice she often seemed to make. She was once to join him at a party, where he had looked forward to her meeting people of whom he was proud to know. At the last moment, she chose to entertain a former employer visiting from New York. She justified it by saying he was "brilliant." This man had made a killing by acquiring distressed businesses. After some questioning, Navin learned this stranger's brilliance came from running companies into the ground and pocketing a significant cut of the venture capital he had secured. But as Navin waited dutifully while Audrey curled up to a man she often described as "ambitious," a series of text-messaged updates reiterated Navin's irrelevance. First, her cocktails with the New Yorker turned to dinner. Dinner turned to post-dinner cocktails. Cocktails moved to a trendy new nightclub. After a fifth text message, a dejected Navin called it a night.

Two weeks later, she was invited to a prestigious and exclusive black-tie charity affair and she invited her girlfriend. Navin sat at home and waited for her to stop by. She never did. Alone in the dark, he began to wonder just how irrelevant and inadequate he had become.

Nonetheless, Navin treated Audrey as a princess, and she, an only child, demanded nothing less. Eventually, he came to believe that her sophisticated beauty and tight bodily form had afforded her the taste of a society higher than her own. This was enough, he thought, to form her addiction.

Having come to know her personality as he had, he also had difficulty with the chasm between her theoretical professional acumen and the level of success she seemed to enjoy. Despite her voluptuous beauty, she was quite nebbish; a nerd for her profession and lacking in any appreciation for humor. When she did laugh, it was mostly a snort. But he—and he assumed others, as well—found her rare moments of genuine laughter charming in their awkwardness. It had occurred to him that when middle-aged-fathers-of-three-perpetually-engorged males make business decisions, five-feet-six-inches of voluptuous beauty, a sexy shrug of a single shoulder, a seductive smile and a graceless gasp of a giggle can go a long way. He, too, found her cumbersomeness charming, and used it as a reason to downplay his cynicism of her that quietly irked him.

At that moment on the beach, he knew she was right. He couldn't make enough money. His taking her to Paris for her birthday or to Bermuda for a long weekend would never satisfy her. A two-hundred-and-fifty-dollar meal with a two-hundred-and-fifty-dollar bottle of wine and two-hundred-and-fifty-dollar scalped tickets to a show on a Friday night could never be enough. The thoughtfulness of fresh, hand-delivered flowers each week would always be overshadowed by something that wasn't delivered. Home-cooked meals, a candlelit apartment, access to beach homes, urban high-rise condominiums and mountain retreats. None of it was enough because there would always be more to have. She worked with millionaires. And one billionaire. She was millionaire fringe cozying her way into a lifestyle of prestige and excess. An upstart.

Despite his success, he would never be able to provide what she sought. He was simply not so greedy. He was, however, generous with all he had, especially affection. And he was quick to define it as love.

The offense he took to her shameful lack of gratitude toward his best efforts calmed his reaction on the beach that night. She descried his stoic affront, no matter how manufactured it might had been, and it seemed to sting her.

As rare as her genuine snorted laugh, so too seemed her pain. It looked real. He could see in her eyes that she feared something, perhaps regret. He quickly assumed she was making a painful decision between this greed and love, and hoped this notion would act as salve for his burn.

Not so long ago, Navin's mind would have raced to construct and deliver an emblazed auditory barrage designed to be nothing but hurtful. It was an old, destructive habit of his. When the war was lost, he often nuked the landscape. But everything that came to mind suddenly seemed beneath him to say.

"I'm sorry," she continued. "That came out harsh."

"No, Audrey, it—" he began.

"No, I mean it's your ambition," she said. "When we met, I thought I had met this wonderfully ambitious man. And here we are."

"Well, you did meet him, and here we are," he said. "But it's a matter of what we're ambitious for."

The pair looked to the sand, the sky and the ocean. They looked everywhere but at each other.

"It's time you face an ugly truth, and that is your

heart is being run by things not from the heart," he said. "And I guess you had to beat me to the punch in letting me go before I did the same to you. But, Audrey, you are not going to be happy until you stop being so self-absorbed." He paused for a moment. He felt a surge of electricity race from the base of his spine to the nape of his neck. His next words, he immediately recognized, were spot on: "No man you think is worth your time is going to put up with your shit."

With that, he turned and began the walk to her beach house. She, speechless, watched him take a few steps. She took a step to follow, stopped, and began to walk after him.

"I just want *more*," she said.

It wasn't clear to him that she had the capacity to understand what he had said. His gut said she hadn't. He reasoned that if she could take his words to heart, then she could embrace the love he offered. No matter how frightened he was, for the first time in his life he dropped all defenses to give someone all he had to give. But he felt his fears were realized—his all wasn't good enough, at least for her.

He knew that what he said was his first admission of disliking a significant part of her, yet against reason, he had said it in hopes to have her change her mind and stay.

When they reached his car in the beach home's driveway, she said, "I do love you, Navin."

He tucked his fingers beneath the handle of his car's door and pulled his hand outward slightly so that his fingertips hung on the handle's lip. Then he stopped to think of his choices: He wanted so much to stay, to convince her he was worthwhile. But he wanted to put as much effort into his pride as he had put into treating her so well.

Facing his options, he was struck with the realization that each physical action into the car was a step closer to never seeing her again. First, he would open the door. Then, get in the car. Put the key into the ignition. Start the car. And then they would be finished. One thing was certain: Navin's stubbornness guaranteed that once he pulled away, he would never look back.

Unwilling to begin the final sequence, he held his hand still for a moment, and then let it drop to his side. He turned to face her. "Audrey, I learned a long time ago not to talk anyone out of what they say they want," he said. "When I leave, I am gone. I will not call. You love me. Will you take a step back and try to make this work?" Their eyes remained locked. He sighed. He tilted his head. He intensified his stare as if he thought he could control her answer. "Yes or no?" he asked.

Audrey erupted into to tears. "I'm sorry," she said. "No." The clef in her chin disappeared behind the trembling of sadness.

And with that, he gave her the benefit of the doubt. He believed she did love him. She had said so. He believed she did think he was amazing. She had said so. He believed that she wanted things he couldn't provide. She had said that, as well. But what she didn't say was that she was unable to accept love. She was unable to hold her tongue. To appreciate. To place others before her. To treat him or others with respect. To be intimate. To be affectionate. He now believed she punted. A forfeit is easier than playing and losing. He thought that she belonged in that world she sought, something short of meaningful, and for a moment, he pitied her.

Later, he would feel he had been used. He would determine that he was disposable. He would soon grow angry. But no matter how he felt about her quandary, he knew she had wasted his time.

He gave her a nod and without a kiss, without a hug and without a touch, he turned to get into his car.

"I do love you," she sobbed. "You deserve better.

You are amazing."

"You've lost a pretty good one this time," he said as he scraped the bottom for the last of his self-esteem.

"I know," she said, hardly audible.

He opened the driver's side door and tossed his overnight bag across the driver's seat onto the opposite floorboard. He climbed into his car and started the engine. He closed his door and backed out the driveway onto the street. Navin had forced his brain to command his body to take this series of dreaded steps.

Without looking back at her, he drove off into the darkness of an unlit beach road. Immediately, he became a scathing critic of himself. "You asked the wrong fucking question," he said aloud. "You ask, 'Yes or no?'" The hum of the car filled the cabin and he tapped the top of the steering wheel with the side of his thumb. "Why not ask, 'Say yes?', you idiot?"

One mile from Audrey's beach house, Navin's car ran out of gas.

CR

"FORE!" Sir Winston Churchill yelled. His golf ball flew well left of his target and dropped between an elderly man and woman on the next tee. The woman, about seventy, turned and gave Winston the finger.

"That really sucked," Navin said. "You've been trying to kill them all day."

"I suppose I have," Winston said. "At least you're down the middle."

"Yup," Navin said. "That's what happens when the ball doesn't get airborne."

"What happens?" Winston asked.

"Consistency," Navin said.

Winston was dressed quite casually for a golf outing with his friend, Navin. He wore olive-green cargo pants cut off just below the knees, and sandals on his feet. Loose strands of silver back hair rose and escaped from beneath the collar of his vintage Iron Maiden concert t-shirt. The front of his shirt draped over his belly, presumably leaving the bottom side of his gut exposed to the open air. A Nike swoosh logo-brandished sun visor shielded his eyes, but left the top of his head exposed to the high midday sun. He had not shaven in days, but his stubbly beard was hardly detectable from more than a few feet away. He wore a golf glove on each hand.

The pair lifted their golf bags and slapped them across their backs to retrieve their balls. Navin, in a plain white t-shirt, plaid shorts and untied white sneakers, had only a few steps to go and soon he would be addressing his second shot.

"Why did you even use the shoulder strap?" Winston asked. "Not that far of a walk."

"Dunno, really," Navin said.

The golf course was a small, nine-hole layout that occupied a square parcel of land in the middle of a mature and charming neighborhood. It wasn't Florida. It wasn't New York. In fact, neither Navin nor Sir Winston knew where it was. The homes looked older. The landscape was green. The cars were nice but not luxurious.

"Where are we?" Navin asked as he looked around.

"Not sure," Winston said. "Probably in one of your dreams."

Navin looked to his left and then to his right. "Oh, yeah, probably." He selected a nine iron, dropped his bag away from his ball and began to assess his next shot. "How far, you think?" he asked the former prime minister and accomplished orator.

"Let's see," Winston said. "From the tee the hole played one hundred-thirty yards, and so you hit it about twenty yards, so I'd say about one hundred-thirty yards."

"Still?" Navin asked.

"Tall weeds," Winston said. "Bad lie."

Navin gripped his club and took a position that placed the ball between him and the green. To his left, he saw the elderly couple that Winston had nearly maimed moments before. Directly ahead lay the uneven and splotchy fairway of an underfunded community golf course. To his right, an embankment lifted subtly to a height of about twenty feet. The slope was dotted with a handful of saplings that stood with the aid of wooden stakes. Two or three larger trees rose high enough to suggest a boundary. A neighborhood street rode along the top of the embankment. Parked cars lined the curb on the opposite side of the street. Beyond the cars rested front yards that featured magnolia trees of impressive girth, rose bushes in full bloom, ivy-clung trellises and a variety of brightly specked flower beds that rolled along like elaborately carpeted porches for the older, red-bricked, two-story homes that backed them.

"Are you still in New York right now?" Winston asked.

"Yup," Navin said.

"Sleeping?" Winston asked.

"We're playing golf, aren't we?" Navin said.

"How's the trip this time?"

"The same, really. It's a lonely place, but I like it for some reason."

"Every place is a lonely place for you, Navin," Winston said. "But you got an award, I hear!"

"True," Navin said. "I did. That fat bastard Simon tricked me. But it's the city. I feel less lonely in my lonesomeness there. Foolish, I know." He addressed his ball and looked toward the pin. He began to waggle his club.

"The greatest lesson in life is to know that even fools are right sometimes," Winston said.

Navin stopped and stepped back. "Is that one of yours?" he asked.

"Yes, son, it is."

"I thought it was Will Rogers."

"No, sir. Mine."

"Hmm."

Navin readdressed his ball and paused for a moment. He snapped his club back and around his body, over his head, then rushed the club face downward and struck the ball. The ball arced upward. It lofted high into the air and began to bend to the right and toward the street atop the ridge. They watched as the ball dropped just to the left of the rear quarter panel of a parked car. On its upward rebound, it struck the bottom of the vehicle and rattled several times before resting against the curb beneath the car's right rear tire.

Winston gave a look to the car, and then to Navin. "Now, this is not the end," he said. "It is not even the beginning of the end. But it is, perhaps, the end of the beginning."

Navin, still in his posed follow through, dropped his arms and looked at Winston. "Groucho Marx?" he asked.

"No," Winston said. "Me, again."

Navin walked to his bag, bent over, grasped the top and lifted it upright. He slid his nine iron into the bag and slung the bag over his shoulder. "I'm terrible at this," he said.

"Golf is a game whose aim it is to hit a very small ball into an even smaller hole with weapons singularly ill-designed for the purpose," Winston said.

"Are you quoting yourself again?" Navin asked.

"Yup." Winston said. "Have you surfed the Net? I am very, *very* quotable."

"Do you have any bowling quotes?" Navin asked.

"Don't think so."

"Then let's go bowling."

"What?"

"This is going to be an entire dream of Winston Churchill quotes that I didn't even know I knew, and I am going to wake up wondering how I knew them," Navin said.

"Not at all, Navin," Winston said. "This dream is going to spiral out of control and hit you right in the face with some subject matter that will leave you more confused and lonelier than you were yesterday."

The two walked up the incline to retrieve Navin's ball from beneath the car. Winston stopped at the top of the hill and stood next to a golden retriever that was lying on the cool grass. Navin crossed the street. A small figure stood up from behind the car and startled him. It was Audrey. She was in black-and-white Ed Hardy jogging attire and sported unblemished white running shoes with silver embellishments. Her left forearm bent sharply up from the elbow. The handle of a plastic bucket hung from her arm. The bucket was half full of golf balls she, Navin presumed, had collected during her stroll around the golf course.

"Audrey!" Navin said.

"Oh," she said. "Hi, Navin."

He looked her up and down and noticed she held his ball in her right hand. "I think you've picked up my ball."

"No. I don't think so. I found this ball."

"Where?"

"There," she said pointing toward the right-rear tire of the parked car.

"Yes," he said. "That's my ball. I just hit it."

"No, Navin, it's not."

"It *is*, Audrey. Can I have it, please?"

She looked at the ball, and back at him. "What were you hitting?"

"You need for me to identify my ball? A fucking Titleist, I don't know—"

"The number?"

"You're kidding."

"It's golf, Navin. You have to know what you hit."

"It cost nine dollars to play this piece-of-shit course," he said. "Golf etiquette hardly applies."

"Then if you can't prove it's your ball, then it's not your ball." She held it above her bucket for a split second then let it drop. She turned to walk away.

"What the fuck?" he asked. "Fuck you, Audrey!" he yelled.

She turned and screamed, "What?"

"Fuck *you!*"

She grabbed a ball from the bucket and threw it at him. He jumped up, and then dove. His golf bag slipped from his shoulder and crashed to the ground. His golf clubs spilled from the bag into the street. She pulled a second ball from the bucket, threw it, and this time hit him in the side of the head.

"What?" he yelled. "Not even a thank you?"

"For meatballs, Navin?" she yelled. "Homemade meatballs?" She took another ball from the bucket and threw it at him. "I think if I keep looking, I'll find your ball . . ."

"Yeah, for meatballs, and travel, and love . . .," he said, and then ducked as a golf ball sailed over his head. "And fresh flowers on Fridays, and listening to your drawn-out stories about your rich, crooked friends, and how well you fit in with them, and how smart they all think you are." A fourth golf ball grazed his ear and, in his attempt to elude it, he tripped on a golf club and fell to the ground.

"Navin," Winston said from across the road. "Men occasionally stumble over truth, but most of them pick themselves up and hurry off as if nothing ever happened."

Navin picked himself up from the ground and, with knees and elbows scraped from the pavement, looked to Winston unappreciatively. As he did, a golf ball hit him in his left elbow. "*Jesus!*" he said.

"You sure are proud of your efforts with us," she

yelled as she reached for another ball. "Eh, Navin?"

"Well, yes!" he said as two balls in quick succession bounced toward and then past him. "Shouldn't I be?"

"Navin," Winston beckoned calmly.

"*What?*" Navin snapped.

"A fanatic is one who can't change his mind and won't change the subject," Winston said.

"I get it!" Navin said. "You're *quotable!*"

"I took it, Navin," Audrey said as she pulled another ball from the bucket. "I took it because you gave it."

Navin backpedaled, but she stalked him with her arsenal of dimpled projectiles.

"Audrey," Winston said. "We make a living by what we get; we make a life by what we give." He quickly ducked as a golf ball cruised past his head.

"Oh, fuck *off*, Churchill," she said. Her perfect olive face had turned reddish now.

Sensing she was still attacking, Navin picked a club from the ground and, wielding it as a weapon, began to storm her position. She saw that his momentum would not be hindered by the rate at which she was able to throw golf balls. She held both hands up to signal a cease fire.

"I don't have to thank you for the wine, and the food, and the concern," she said. "It's who you are, Navin. You did nothing special for me. You were just you." And she turned and walked away.

"I did nothing special because I was just me?" he said barely aloud to himself. "Holy shit."

He stood frustrated and angry and torn. The street was littered with golf clubs and a dozen or so golf balls. He squatted then sat in the street amongst the orphaned golf equipment. In a flash, he remembered all of the ways he showed his thoughtfulness: his concern for her health; his patience for her new dog and new business; his willingness to establish finish lines so that when she was ready to resume with him, he would be ready; the times when he had nothing to say to her except, "I miss you, Audrey." And he did truly miss her.

He sat with blood trickling from scrapes on his knees and soon noticed the clattering of the dog's footsteps on pavement growing near. It sat next to Navin and looked straight ahead to the golf course. It reared its head back to its right, leaned its body to the left, and began to scratch its right ear with its right hind leg. Its tag read "Sophie," and it jingled as it scratched. When it was done, it stood up, reached to Navin and licked him twice on the cheek. Then it walked away.

Winston stood amused and turned to walk down the

hill to retrieve his own golf ball. "Outside of a dog, a book is a man's best friend," Winston said. "Inside of a dog, it's too dark to read."

"You've got a quote for everything, don't you?" Navin asked.

"No," Winston said. "That one was Groucho Marx."

ଓ

Morning sunlight washed over Smith & Wollensky's, along 49th Street, and through the curtains of Navin's room, over his feet and torso, and landed on his closed eyelids. He awoke peacefully and though something hung on his mind, he thought how this might have been the best night's sleep he had had in a while. He gazed to the clock on the nightstand and his satisfaction turned to disappointment. It was just 6:18 a.m. It was too early. This day, therefore, would be longer than most.

He quickly fell introspective. There had been a dream. He thought the dream had played out as a movie, but he could not recall the plot. He sorted through what he could recall and identified four new insights: One, he hated golf and he was not good at it. Two, he had memorized more Churchill quotations than he had ever realized. Three, Audrey was a sponge that soaked in whatever was presented to her, and she was oblivious and uncaring as to how it might look to Winston Churchill. Four, he was a sucker.

He rolled his eyes and turned to notice the void to his left—a void that until just weeks before had been filled by Audrey—and felt foolish some more.

Mornings were the hardest part of his days. No matter how trying a day might have been, waking the next morning with Audrey felt as though the universe had pressed a giant reset button. It was his biggest asset, but yet biggest curse: He could start over each day, but it would cost him the perspective of the past. The rest of the world, however, was keeping score, and he was often unpleasantly surprised by the outcome.

Again, he had no place to be. Wide awake and alone with his thoughts, he lay in bed doing all he could to keep morning emptiness from setting the tone for his day. As proud as he was of himself for his strong exit from Audrey's life, the alone times jumbled his reality and his perceptions, and left him searching for ways to belittle him. In her case, he simply could not reconcile all he gave with how badly she made him feel. But today, he was in New York.

He loved New York. To him, the city was an obvious-but-unidentified sum of its noise, mass of humanity and rhythm. It inspired his imagination to run wild and his logic to grow keen. It stirred the thinker within and provided opportunity, if not escape.

Sensing an unwelcome introspective day caused by a ridiculous dream he could hardly recall, he jumped from bed determined to change his mood's path. He went to the window and looked out to the New York City morning. He organized the clothes he had strewn across the room the night before. He drifted into the bathroom and, oblivious to his reflection in the mirror, brushed his teeth. He returned to the bedroom and looked to Steve Martin's journal. He wondered how he might return it.

Without an answer, he flopped back onto the bed. Quickly, the injustice he felt beneath the Audrey breakup resurfaced and began to bubble over. "Sixteen-million people outside those windows," he thought, "and I'm living with this ghost."

He sighed, and his eyes scanned the room and fell upon his laptop. He rose from the bed, retrieved his computer, crashed back onto his bed and opened it. He began to compose an email to his friend Sid:

From: "Navin R. Johnson"
Sent: 01/30/2013 09:09 AM EST
To: Sid Smalls
Subject: getting it off my chest . . .

Navin was faced with a blank white box and the task of tackling something he seldom took on. He saw this box as an ear—Sid's ear. He was free to write all he wanted. Though he normally wouldn't, today he did:

"Just venting. No need to read, no need to respond . . . I don't get it. Everything was going great . . . Amazing. My flaws? The same ones. But I worked hard. I pushed them way down. Her flaws? More on that later, MUCH more. But normal woman stuff . . . if I told her there was something I needed she would give me the all-chick, all-powerful "If I am such a horrible person . . ." defense designed to blow the Titanic out of the water, take logical discussion and accountability out of the picture, and instill fear in anyone who dares a dialogue that would better the whole picture. So I dropped it. Quickly . . ."

And so it began. His fingers pecked furiously and his

eyes never scanned the email for typos or grammar. He wrote unconsciously and incessantly. He followed a first anecdote of his thoughtfulness with another anecdote, and then another, and then another. He built a case for his value as her companion by citing the happiness of her parents, and by describing what he had captured in pictures while in Europe with her. He defended himself as if he were on trial. As he proved his own value, his stories began to reveal her unflattering side. He realized he was exposing himself as deeply bitter. It was perhaps, he thought, another overdue admission:

"I knew then this was going to be a bad thing for us . . ."

"Plus, she had intimacy issues. Not with sex . . . sex was amazing. But affection . . ."

"With her new clients came more and more events . . ."

"She has this one particular smile for me that I know is real and that was the last time I saw that smile . . ."

The words flowed into sentences, which flowed into

paragraphs, which flowed into pages upon pages of text—a great wall of text the size of China's.

A dozen or more anecdotes piled on to create an epic tale. Scenes appeared chronologically. And then, ultimately, the final act. He wrote, in great detail, about the breakup and dialogue on the beach. His analysis followed that account and, predictably, the email circled around and wove into a scathing review of her essence:

> "So here is what I know: She is embarrassed when I dance, snaps at a moment's notice over simply not hearing me, is completely self-absorbed, doesn't think anyone knows how important she is or how hard it is to be so important, has no real sense of humor, is not much of a deep thinker, is not accountable and is a very self-reverent excuse maker, doesn't get Steve Martin, will choose anyone's point of view over her boyfriend's on principle I guess, places way too much stock in her image at every turn, is unable to enjoy me enjoying something and rather just criticizes me for enjoying things that she doesn't get, never provides the benefit of the doubt, will not take on anything that is a challenge, always assumes the worst, is driven

completely by money and the prospect that a husband will be more of a partner than a soul mate, has very little to hang her hat on, therefore inflates that self-worth to unreal proportion and has such low self-esteem that everything is a threat . . . everything. And she is naïve, which is such a contradiction to what she thinks she is and what she thinks she wants."

His declaration had grown severe and comprehensive. But, after a barrage of thousands of words, he summed it up simply:

"I did this right. I worked hard this time. I want credit. If you read all this, thanks, Sid. Navin."

Only when he had finished did he realize just how much he had written and how much time had passed. He read it again, and then once more. Then his concern turned toward Sid. He felt as though sending something so lengthy was an intrusion. But despite tired eyes, he felt a certain relief.

Navin had written the early morning away. Hunger had snuck up on him. He leapt up, gathered his room key from the bathroom vanity and left to go eat. Over breakfast and now with a purged brain, he thought he would plot his search for Steve Martin.

BARSTOOLS | 4

NAVIN HAD CONFIDED in Sid to try and find peace of mind. It seemed to have worked, for now, and so he looked to the promise of an impromptu and absurd adventure.

Normally on such trips, he would read the New York Times over breakfast. But since placing his order, he had lost his patience for idling. He nervously and relentlessly tapped his foot against his table's base. This annoyed the neighboring elderly woman—the same elderly woman he annoyed the day before in the elevator car—seated at a table to his left. She rolled her eyes.

As breakfast arrived, he asked for his check and a splash of fresh coffee. To save time, he ate only the good parts—two over-easy egg yolks, bacon, and a half-slice of toast with strawberry jam—then signed the check to his room. He left a generous and unthinking eight-dollar gratuity on an eighteen-dollar tab. Navin gathered his copy of the Times, which had been left at Room 612's door before dawn, and returned to his room.

The room was filled with the warmth from mid-morning sunlight amplified through the window panes. Housekeeping had yet to make the room, so the towels from his morning shower still littered the bathroom floor. The open and unflushed toilet gave witness to his zeal to begin his day. With nothing really to gather—his room key, wallet and phone were already in his pockets—he left his room to hunt Steve Martin.

"Taxi, sir?" the Marriott doorman asked.

"Umm, I . . . don't know," Navin said. He had no idea how to begin his quest. He had not, until now, even thought of it. He gave a squint upward to an unending blue sky and said, "I think I'll walk. The sun is warm."

The deception that brought him to New York for an unexpected and uncomfortable honor also gave him time with the city with which he shared an affair. Like many recent trips here, there was no business to be done. But on previous trips, he would pack a tidy black suit and tie as a reminder of how he could profit from his trips to New York. He held an exquisite taste in wardrobe. But on this trip, his taste and reminder hung in a closet in Florida.

Business had introduced him to the borough and he had, essentially, left business for Manhattan. With each trip he would get to know her better—the city's quirks and rhythms, her vulnerabilities and strengths. Each visit melded him more into the city's landscape. His obsession for her caused him to avoid firm schedules when he visited. Appointments were made and not kept. Contacts grew faint. But meetings and contacts were always required to justify his visits to Gotham.

The charade often began with an email to a contact or two announcing his impending visit to the city. "Perhaps we could chat then," he would suggest. Contrived scheduling conflicts and imaginary complications caused most of the schedule he did have to evaporate. He would be left with nothing other to do than to court the city.

Until now. The possession of Steve Martin's journal had given him and his love for New York a worthy cause. Seeking the Holy Grail was one thing. Returning the Holy Grail to its owner was quite the other.

"A Village Voice and a New Yorker," he muttered aloud as he walked south down Lexington Avenue. A cup of coffee, he reasoned, would allow him time to relax and merge into Manhattan's rhythm. The stillness of a coffee would complement the perusal of periodicals for hints as to why Steve Martin could be in town and, most relevant, where he might be.

He passed an empty Village Voice newspaper box on his way to a newsstand where he bought the week's New Yorker. After pocketing his change, he rolled the magazine into a baton and carried it in his fist. Blocks later, he found a paper box that held four copies of The Village Voice. He snagged one copy and was now ready to settle into a coffee shop for a cup and some involved research. As he set his sights on locating a coffee shop, he checked the time. It was 11:11. He paused and grinned. After a moment, he resumed his walk and searched for a counter and a stool to claim as his.

Absent a coffee shop along his path, Navin found an attractive bar and restaurant. Workers in white smocks and aprons hurried to prepare for a sizable lunch rush. Through the entryway, the dining room opened to the right. The room featured stoic, dark-wood tables in symmetrical formations topped with white tablecloths, flatware and white napkins that formed small tents. The tables were prepared to welcome business meetings, girl-only-playing-hooky lunch dates, and the occasional meeting between an executive and his mistress. Navin imagined this food hall would bear witness to a thousand or more "I-am-leaving-her-this-weekend" promises.

To the left of the entryway was a long, weighty bar. Liquor bottles were brightly lit from above and backed by a mirror. The mirror angled downward and would later reveal the bald spots on many of the men who dined in the dining room. He spotted an open stool at the end of the bar and claimed the prime coffee-drinking, magazine-reading and notice-and-be-noticed spot.

He was an able observer and mimic. He had always noticed that those who occupied the spot at the end of a crowded bar had something to read, a peculiar-looking cigarette to smoke, a funny or quirky hat, and an all-knowing grin. He was keenly aware that he had left his hat in his room; smoking in public places had been banned in New York City years before; and any grin he might try to show would only come off as cocky in the worst case, and as counterfeit in the most pathetic case. All he had, then, were two magazines and a desire to drink coffee.

He was sure his early arrival would disrupt a genuine New York denizen's daily routine. This, he rationalized, was this stranger's price to pay for residing in what Navin viewed as the most desirable place to live in the world.

Navin climbed atop his stool and received his coffee just as the first of the lunchtime patrons began to file into the restaurant. He paged through the magazines he had collected in a search for clues. The pastime of people watching, however, was far more enticing. He alternately looked directly into the restaurant and up to the mirror for the unique view it provided. As his ability to concentrate on the hunt for Steve Martin waned, Navin tried to guess which patrons were executives accompanied by their mistresses. He quickly surmised that any man and woman alone at a table were indulging in the latest chapter of their exciting secret lives together. There were no exceptions. As for the rest of the guests, he wasn't that interested.

Reaching this conclusion resolved a question and returned his attention more fully to his magazines. With his coffee now nearly half gone, he recklessly paged through The Village Voice. He feared that such a publication at such a prestigious stool at the bar defied the very image Navin felt he wanted to mimic. If his elusive, all-knowing grin wasn't giving him away, then acting as if he didn't notice the escort service ads near the back of the tabloid probably was. He folded the magazine once, then twice over, and looked up to notice that no one was noticing him.

The waiter warmed Navin's coffee, and Navin gave him an appreciative nod. He leaned to one side to slide the Voice beneath him to sit on it for safekeeping. He knew that once the Voice was gone, it was gone for the week. He had, after all, snagged one of the only four copies he had run across.

With a fraudulent swagger, he opened The New Yorker to the "Goings On About Town" page that often reported skeletal details about arts-related events and openings in the city. The capsules often mentioned celebrities who were expected to appear around the city, and its cultural happenings. Steve Martin was a periodic contributor to The New Yorker, which is why Navin subscribed to the magazine years before. At one point, he wondered why he subscribed to an entire magazine to predominantly rush to the "Shouts & Murmurs" page.

The subscription became much more to him than that, however. It was displayed on his coffee table at home, and often took residence in his bathroom. When his patience and diligence allowed, he enjoyed the magazine's quiet, insightful and poignant reporting and opinion on paramount global issues. But more than anything, the magazine was a weekly love letter or portrait from the object of his infatuation: All who visited him could see an issue or two lying about his apartment and assume New York City and Navin were romantically involved. But for today, if there were any events in Manhattan that Steve Martin might attend, Navin hoped they would be listed in The New Yorker.

His eyes darted between the magazine's pages and back up to the mirror that served as a window to a world of infidelity. Occasionally, he peered upward to mistakenly recognize someone as a celebrity. Moments after his first cup was refilled, he had thought he had seen (and quickly realized he had not seen) Ethan Hawke, Harrison Ford, Russell Brand and a little redheaded kid with a lisp whom he could not name. All Navin knew was that he used to appear on Mike Douglas' daytime-television show in the 1970s.

Navin loved the city because New York was full of, well, New York moments. In a city of 16 million people, anything was possible. It is, despite the mass of humanity that inhabits it, the smallest community in the world. He viewed the island of Manhattan as a fishbowl. Every skyscraper and building was a sunken plastic treasure chest or a bubbly windmill. If one swam around them enough, one would eventually run into the same school of tetra. Like a fishbowl, no one ever really got out. If they did, no one noticed because they always came back. In New York, no one seemed to care what happened in the meantime.

New York was his romantic ideal. He always thought he would meet his love here. Or his purpose. Or his death. Or his heroism. Or himself.

Of late, he was titillated by the prospect—or at least the fantasy—that his present might intersect with his past to create a romantic and just future. It would be an improbable-but-everlasting convergence that, he reasoned, could only happen in New York. As he slurped another sip, that thought left his mind. He glanced to the restaurant and saw Audrey being seated at one of the few empty tables in the room. This was not the romantic notion of which he had dreamt.

☙

Navin required closure, and closure could only occur in the presence of reason. The abstract made him uneasy. Peace of mind was impossible without answers. "Broken hearts," he once advised a grieving friend, "are not the result love lost, but more from the void of logic that surrounds the situation." To him, it was the unreasonable that caused the pain. It's the shock of losing something that should be retained. It's the need for a better outcome when one thinks they are doing their best. "If you can admit you sucked at this relationship, then it's far easier to let go with a lot less anguish," he told his friend.

But as impressed as he was with his own clinical insight that night many years ago, he had never experienced a loss firsthand—not at that point, at least. It was insight that he would give to countless others that followed, and it always seemed to help. Like a doctor who could give painful shots to a patient because he didn't feel the pain himself, Navin's view on life and love was detached. He had never known the very real pain caused by rejection, the confusion triggered by being lost without direction, or being emotionally homeless. Consequence was only a concept.

He was a fabled listener for those in need to bare their souls, an ear when they hurt, or a baseline of logic. His willingness and ability to defuse an emotional situation made him a reliable friend. He was a friend to all who needed one and was quick with seemingly the right thing to say. He could turn the tides for anyone.

About three years before this day, he had met the first person who needed his help for whom he failed. He met him in his own bathroom, in his own mirror, using his own toothbrush. This person shared his vivid blue eyes. The world woke Navin with the subtle whack of a frying pan to the back of his head.

As Navin was doling out theory on how to reconstruct a broken life, his naivety grew. His own life was falling more deeply asleep. He had never known loss—not through death, or the end of a relationship that he wanted. And so, with no comprehension of risk, his emotions fell numb.

To others, his advice was only his theory and, as the saying goes, "Those who can, do; those who can't, teach." He was the teacher that had yet to be tested.

Audrey was the latest in a series of botched relationships. Navin had been unable to retain a relationship for three years. He did not have the answers for himself that he had always had for others. If he did, he no longer considered himself a credible source. In either case, he had become trapped by his inability to treat himself as well as any friend.

At this moment, his fleeting peace of mind and mission to locate Steve Martin melted into his emotional and uncontrolled thought. The bald heads that spotted the mirror behind the bar blurred into a whitened landscape.

The magazines he collected were reduced to ruins of fruitless fancy. His morning of New York moments was dwarfed by emotions best described as a rat's nest of intertwined rubber bands in a cellophane baggie.

And there in the restaurant, sixteen-hundred miles from home, his past did intersect with his present.

Navin vowed to never query Audrey for answers. But he did require a "thank you." He felt he deserved her confession that, since her materialistic-driven dismissal of Navin, her nights had been full of tears and loneliness and uncertainty and restless frustration. He yearned for fate to intervene. He longed for Audrey—in the most unexpected and improvised setting—to see him and melt with love and regret.

"Navin," he wished to hear her say with trembled voice. "I was wrong, it was a mistake. Please, can we talk?"

He longed to say, "Audrey, no."

This longing quickly turned into a swirling fantasy as he sat at the bar. An alternate reality consumed him. The lunch crowd's buzz morphed into the white noise that floated Navin to the table at which she sat.

"Audrey," he said.

She looked away from her lunch date and turned to see Navin. "Navin!" she blurted.

"You know my friend, Steve Martin?" he asked.

She moved her eyes from Navin to the well-dressed man with the household face that stood to Navin's left. "Pleasure, Mr. Martin," she said. "I had no idea you—"

"Likewise," Steve interrupted.

"Audrey is the one I have been telling you about, Steve," Navin said.

Steve rocked to the balls of his feet and clasped his hands behind his back. He tilted his head back and tightened his lips. "I seeeeee," he said.

"Why are you in town, Navin?" Audrey said.

"Why are *you* in town?" Steve interrupted.

"Well, I have a—" she began.

"A what? A what?" Steve pressed. "A date with someone who makes enough money for you? Hmmm?"

She was clearly offended and glared at Navin. "You told *Steve Martin?*" she grunted.

"Why wouldn't I, Audrey?" Navin said in a higher-pitched voice. "Steve Martin is my friend. Friends tell friends things."

"Yes, Audrey," Steve said. "Friends tell friends things."

"Well, I hope it was within context, Navin," she said. "I know how badly that whole ambition and money thing could sound if it's taken out of context."

"I'll give you context, missy," said Steve at a level that caught the restaurant's attention. "You are a little gold-digging farm animal whose sole purpose is to be the princess you think you are, but when it comes right down to it you are probably a lousy lay and will make a terrible mother."

Just then, Steve was interrupted by an excited autograph seeker who extended a pen and a napkin. "Could you please, sir?" the smallish woman asked.

"Now *that's* context," he continued toward Audrey. He took the fan's napkin and pen without breaking his gaze from Audrey. "You money-grubbing, goat-sucking swine!" he groaned and, with his elbow remaining tight to his side, whipped the autographed napkin back to the awestruck fan.

"Thanks, Mr. Martin," said the woman.

"My pleasure, ma'am," Steve said through clinched teeth, and with a squinted stare that landed directly upon Audrey. "I happen to be fresh out of my pre-autographed cards."

"Steve, please," Navin said. "I appreciate it, but . . ."

Steve slowly turned to Navin, cocked his head and said calmly, "Navin, I'll handle this." Turning back to Audrey, he continued. "He made you homemade meatballs, Audrey. How do you sleep at night? *Really*."

Steve did a double take when he noticed the well-dressed and handsome man seated across the table from her. Though attractive, his eyes lacked a charisma she often sought. He was obviously embarrassed, but certainly entertained by Steve Martin's tirade.

"Who are you?" Steve asked the man.

"I'm Robert," he said.

"Did you bring your tax return for her review, Bobbo?" Steve asked.

Robert paused. "It's Robert, Mr. Martin." He turned to her. "Audrey, is that why you asked me to bring my tax records?"

"I *knew* it!" Steve shouted as he pointed.

"Well, a girl's got to be sure, honey," she said to Robert.

"You never asked me for my tax returns," Navin said.

"Well, I could tell you didn't have what I wanted," she said.

"How did you know that?" he asked.

"You wore the same sport coat three dates in a row," she said. "I told you I was a fashion plate. This is my fourth date with Robert. Fourth sport coat."

Robert sat quietly, and Navin assumed he was hoping

to conceal the fact that he owned just four sport coats.

"For the record, missy," Steve said, "where I come from we don't measure a man by his bank account, or his earning capacity, or how many sport coats he owns."

"Where do you come from, Steve?" she asked.

"L.A.," Steve said.

"Me, too, and yes, we do," she said.

"Oh, now that you mention it . . .," Steve trailed off. "But still, I don't like you. You are a big, green poop." He turned away and walked back to the corner of the bar to await Navin.

Navin looked to Audrey. "Steve is a good man," he said. "I found his journal and returned it to him. That's how we met." He turned to Robert and said, "I will tell you what one of Audrey's old boyfriends told me—Ken, I think his name was—and that was this: 'I hope you're up for it.'"

Navin returned to his barstool to finish his coffee. He took a sip and felt a smile spread across his face. He was still alone. He noticed the woman who looked from behind like Audrey rise to go to the ladies' room.

He paid the check and walked outside. He checked his watch, and the time was 1:01. The time of day had made him smile once again.

CLOCKS | 5

NAVIN HAD ALWAYS heard that when one caught the time on a clock and the same digits appeared on both sides of the colon, it was the best time to make a wish. He often caught himself avoiding cracks as he walked along sidewalks, lifting his feet as he drove over railroad tracks and making a wish on the first star he spotted on a clear evening. Wishing upon a star was as close to a prayer as the agnostic-leaning Navin would get. Lifting his feet over railroad tracks served as a reminder that doing the occasional sit up might make him feel better about himself. He avoided stepping on cracks more from boredom on long walks rather than to save on his mother's chiropractic bill.

The time of day superstition, however, had taken on paramount meaning. It had seemed that over the past eight months, he was catching the clock just right eighty percent of the time. The odds of this phenomenon occurring within an hour, he reasoned, were one in sixty. The odds to hit it several times within a single day must extrapolate to impossible. He further reasoned the odds to hit it several times in a day, for several days in a row, for several months in a row . . . well, this must mean something.

Navin and Audrey had met about eight months before. On their fifth date, he dusted off his Scrabble board and lit about fifty candles. He ordered a Chinese Thanksgiving. At meal's end, he offered her a choice of four fortune cookies. She chose, and then he chose from the remaining three. The fortune within her chosen cookie was cliché and forgettable. She rolled her eyes as she crunched the cookie into a powder. But his fortune, on the other hand, shook his earth:

"Faith is the answer to peace of mind."

To a man who had suffered a jarring crisis in all realms of faith—faith in himself, a god, any possible universe, or anyone else—this timely message delivered from a fortune cookie on the brink of a promising love affair grabbed him by his throat. On its own, it seemed a delightful omen to recount later, maybe as part of a wedding toast someday.

A quick and unintended glance at the cable box, however, took this small strip of paper and turned it into a scripture as significant to him as the discovery of the Dead Sea Scrolls was to Christianity.

The time was 8:08.

He had lost all faith in all he held dear over the past thirty months. His agnostic slant was swerving into something more drastically alienating. This strange blend of hope and timing and confluence of circumstance had a most profound effect on his state of mind.

Perhaps his fledgling relationship with Audrey heightened his senses for him to accept a positive sign. The sorest of eyes had caught an overdue glimpse of a flickering light. He saw a hopeful end to a ruthless losing streak. These things made him want to accept a higher power. He grew warm thinking this force might be looking out for him. He had looked skyward for such a long time, and all that truly mattered was that the clouds might be parting. His only explanation for this agglomerate of signs and events was that the universe was letting him know it was paying attention.

Though he didn't recognize it then, every clock anyplace in the world from that moment on could deliver this message: *Faith is the answer to peace of mind.*

And so, through his relationship with Audrey—and through its end, and now in the midst of its aftermath—Navin's reminders of his newly found faith—every digital timepiece in the world—spoke to him up to eight times daily.

He eventually believed that the universe drew his eyes to the time displays on his laptop's screen, his microwave or roadside bank signs to counteract his self-destructive thoughts. He was very sad. He felt lost most times. He had painful and mocking dreams. He was certainly depressed and confused. But in his subconscious glances to the nearest clock he was always amazed by, and believed in, the universe's determination to answer his often-hidden and masqueraded calls for help.

He knew that his new time-of-day religion presented itself when it did by design. Audrey was his first serious attempt at a permanent relationship in over a year—a year that saw him court women for the company and sleep with them for their warmth. He had enjoyed a prosperous single life, save a meaningful relationship that had lasted about four years.

Suzy and Navin were, for all intents and purposes, married. He grew bored with her; or, more to the point, he felt she had tired of him. Wanting more, he called it off. It was a slow, numbing breakup. Her desire to hold on to the relationship pushed him farther away. His patience and temper eventually became unbearable—not so much at her, but at himself. He eventually shut her out completely. It would mark the beginning of the end of his naivety.

Months later, he found the acceptance and company he had thrown away in Suzy in his affair with a casual friend's wife. Russell's travels left Jess alone most days each week. Because Navin was sleepwalking through his personal life, and Jess was playing the role of an abandoned married woman, they would inevitably meet for dinner, go to a movie, drink too much, and seek a physical remedy to their confusion and loneliness.

Jess was not particularly attractive to him. Her weight rose and fell in her constant struggle to keep it under control. Once, an unsuspecting friend of Navin's referred to her as Thighasaurus, and Navin genuinely chuckled. Her hygiene was questionable. She had a single, stray black facial hair that she would occasionally trim, but often it would grow to a half-inch long.

Her opinions were generally inane and intractable. She had a passionate disdain for dryer sheets. She abhorred Thanksgiving dinner, and disliked any traditional holiday menu item—especially yams. Sport utility vehicles had to have ski racks or their owners, she assessed, were status-seeking snobs. She hated the people she hung out with, but loved hanging out with them. She wanted a cross-eyed baby because kids in eyeglasses were cute.

Jess could not resolve conflict. Navin once left a party they both attended so that no one could put the pieces together and, on the drive home, received a text message from her that read: "I hate, hate, hate, hate, hate, hate, hate, hate, hate, hate, hate, hate, hate, hate, hate you."

She was not smart. Conversationally, her sense of humor was stale. She was keen on stereotypes. Because she had a limited inventory of real-life anecdotes, she rotated through no more than three stories. Each rendition was laced with as much enthusiasm as the last. One close to her could expect to hear the same tale about every three weeks. Her commentary was typically disagreeable. Sentences usually began with, "Wait, I don't get it." She overused the phrase "Really, are you serious right now," each time she wanted to call to light her self-ordained superiority or judged inferiority of another. Navin's points of enlightenment were rudely dismissed by Jess with a deflating, "Yes, I realize that, but . . ."

She was self-righteous and lazy, but she had nice teeth; was willing to move into a tabooed existence; and she was young—twelve years his junior—and that's all he thought mattered to him.

Russell was a marketing representative for an Asian-based sports-equipment company. His trips, many of which were to his company's base near Tokyo, were often lengthy enough for Navin and Jess to escape on their own journeys. Getaways, in fact, were necessary as to avoid any sightings around town. Key West, Bermuda, Puerto Rico and St. Thomas were all easy two-day getaways from South Florida. Russell's longest trip to Japan, three weeks, allowed Navin and Jess to steal away to Italy for a few days. Manipulating the timing of text-messages and emails helped her orchestrate alibis and communicate with her one or two only friends. In the wee Italian morning hours, she pressed the keys on her phone as Navin slept with his head pressed to her chest.

Her willingness to create this alternate reality allowed him to bring his life to a complete standstill.

Dating wasn't something he particularly enjoyed. Fucking was. And he repaid her by allowing her to tolerate her loneliness while staying married to a very good man.

They had sex nearly every morning and every night. Sex between them was inventive, aggressive and shameless. They would go to any length to please each other, in a moving car, or beneath the blanket on a commercial red-eye flight. He found her desire to be dominated erotic and empowering. She typically preferred a tabletop or kitchen island. Pasta sauce boiling over on the stove while he held her wrists to the hardwood floor and stretched well above her head heightened her ecstasy. And she would think that she raped him, too, most memorably in daylight in the largely uncharted Tuscan hill town of Trequanda, where she pinned him against a handy portion of the village fortification and climbed upon him. It took no more than a couple minutes and when he was through, she fell to the ground. He quickly redressed, then nervously stood sentry as she finished herself with her hand.

For eighteen months, they lived in a passionate, secretive and comfortable parallel dimension. The two, however, differed in that she knew what she was getting from it while he fell deeper into an emotional slumber. He never considered that he might want her as his own wife. She was convenient for him, and the sex was always sublime and often ridiculous. He mistook their ability to confabulate as meaningful dialogue. He misread the apathy he had for his own life as being content. He misunderstood her insatiable sexual appetite for love. He misinterpreted the adventure as life.

Worn from globetrotting and missing his wife, Russell quit his job and took one that required far less travel. Jess went to Navin's apartment and told him that the fervent affair they shared was over. Then she joined him in his shower and took him a final time. It was slow and passionate but it was, in the end, a farewell. Each melded into a sob and embraced under the water's warmth until the shower turned cold. Even then, they refused to let go of each other until they grew too tired to stand.

In the end, Navin never believed Jess felt for Russell as she did Navin. He could only reason that what once was a fun, secretive affair became her prison. The nature of their indiscretion mandated there could be no friends, couples' nights or public sightings. Absent any meaningful dialogue with her, he reasoned that she leaving Russell for him was the most difficult of her options. With Navin relegated to the shadows, she was able to continue the life, friendships and stability Russell and his new job provided.

She had worked too hard, Navin thought, to hide the affair from everyone she knew. A return to a traditional married life with Russell was easy and safe. And so Jess left Navin for her husband.

In doing so, she had carelessly forced Navin to choose his own source of residual pain. The first choice, and the most difficult to resist, was to admit to the affair. This would free himself to pursue her. He knew this would destroy many lives and, inevitably, there would be no victory for him. The second choice—and the one he chose—was to subject himself to a death by a trillion mosquito bites and a billion paper cuts.

He once caught a cable-television show on Chinese water torture. He described to Sid how his mental anguish following the breakup could so easily be compared to the legend. "The show," he told his friend, "concluded that the key was not the regular dropping of water to the forehead. It was the irregularity of the drops that made the torture so effective. The unknowing part of when the next drop would fall."

"Like not knowing when the next thought invades your psyche?" Sid asked.

"And there is no escape from it," Navin said. "And you know what the kicker is?"

"What?"

"The show said cold water made all the difference," Navin said. "Cold water." He had been awoken from his torpidity and simultaneously crushed by a virtual tsunami of ice-cold water, one drop at a time.

And so he, by choosing to fight for Jess in secrecy's vacuum, chose the most frustrating alternative. He committed all he had to convince her to leave Russell without acknowledging their affair to the world. The war for her affection had to be viral. He hadn't a friend on the planet that could help and so, behind the scenes and limited by his desire to protect her, he quickly and inadvertently caused her to grow hateful. He could only present to her a grim option that required character and accountability. He thought she was too young—or too stupid—to hold these traits and she turned on him in the cruelest form: an inability to be honest with him or herself.

She had no real reason to refute him, he thought. He had always treated her beyond her deservedness.

But she was incapable of looking within and admitting to herself that she wanted her cake, and to eat it, too, with neither price nor penalty. But in the end, and despite her esteem for him, he was an acceptable casualty.

"Why not?" he asked in one of their final discussions. "Why not take a chance with me?"

"You had your chance," she said.

"For what?" he asked.

"To ask me to leave him."

"Would you have?"

"We won't know now," she said. After a search with her eyes for something more concrete, she stammered, "Look, I know this will sound selfish and I realize this: I know you have taken me to so many places, but you have never bought me a gift to open."

"A sweater," he snapped, "would have been preferred over Rome?"

He saw that she could not point to anything specific about him that ran her back to Russell. He felt she was simply unwilling to admit to loving him. Storybook scenes they had shared flashed through his mind only to confuse him, causing yet a thousand more, randomly timed drops of cold water to his forehead.

Navin left the restaurant giddy from Steve Martin confronting Audrey before a New York lunch crowd. Though he knew it was a daydream, the serendipitous look to his watch shortly after Steve's assault made Navin feel someone else was in on the joke, even if it really wasn't Steve Martin.

Armed with something that resembled faith, he was ready to tackle an afternoon of nothingness. By 1 p.m., the sun had started to dip below the tops of Manhattan's tallest buildings. The heartless dead-of-winter darkness and chill would soon return. He wanted to eschew the calamity that unfolded the day before—sleeping away the day, and a lonely and downtrodden romp through an artic New York night.

He, on his last night in the city, wanted a fine steak served by a man wearing a coat and tie. A meal accompanied by live jazz being played in a restaurant's dark corner would offer some solace. He hoped to recognize some of the businessmen he had seen lunching with their mistresses now with their wives, and reaffirming their love over expensive fine wine. Smith & Wollensky's unending stare up to his room had broken him.

He still had all afternoon to kill so—with magazines in hand—he headed south toward Union Square. As he walked, he absorbed the day's remaining tolerable temperature. He recalled a small tavern just west of Lexington Avenue and just a couple blocks north of Union Square. His remembering the name wasn't needful for him to find it. He just knew he would recognize the sign that was visible from Lexington Avenue. If he just kept looking to his left at each cross street, a neon beacon would pull him in.

He found the sign, Old Town Bar, right where he remembered it, and entered through the front doors that hung beneath it. Upon entering, he was taken aback by how clean the bar seemed compared to his last visit. He claimed a stool at the bar near the door and realized that he had not been there since a citywide smoking ban was enacted in 2003.

"What'll you have?" asked the bartender.

"A coffee, I guess, to start," Navin said.

Navin looked about, and what he saw freed memories of many drunken nights where Old Town Bar was a regular stop for a single cocktail. Hundreds of frames hung on the walls and crowded each other so tightly that little or no actual wall remained exposed.

They contained vintage newspaper and magazine clippings of sports stories, politicians, and some old vaudevillian acts. The room itself was far longer than it was wide. A single walkway to the rear separated the bar to the left, and booths hugged the wall along the right. The air inside felt old. The wooden bar was rich, dark and cracked. Cobwebs draped the many accessories, and mismatched antiquities surrounded scores of liquor bottles. None of the light fixtures and sconces matched. Most light bulbs were not working, and those that were did not have lampshades. A few sockets hung without light bulbs in them at all.

At the bar's farthest end in the back of the room was a dumbwaiter that was used to deliver the food from a kitchen that was, presumably, one floor above. The rope that suspended the box was thick, and was probably at one time white. Navin cringed at a memory of Old Town Bar: Once, just as he was about to order what looked to be the perfect burger and fries at the best time of night, he noticed mice clinging to the rope that hoisted and lowered the dumbwaiter. The mice scampered around a poor, unsuspecting customer's late-night dinner. Soon after, and with heightened senses, he saw mice making death-defying floor crossings as unsuspecting customers stomped their way to the bar, from the bar, to the restrooms, from the restrooms, and to their dinners that they had left exposed to these tiny denizens.

He remembered thinking that the owners and staff at Old Town Bar must have known about the mice, and perhaps the critters were like the eight dogs owned by a truck stop owner in Nebraska. They all had names, and regulars knew them. And like well-trained dogs, the mice simply knew better than to snack from the paying customer's plate. It was obvious to him some deal had been brokered to prevent these little guys from being exterminated. These mice were not stupid.

He also recalled many nights walking into the crowded bar and the smoke being so thick that he needed to step outside after every drink or two to relieve the sting in his eyes.

"Here you go," the bartender said as he clanked the coffee mug in front of Navin.

"Man," Navin said, "I haven't been here since the smoking ban. Place looks different."

"Yeah," the bartender said. "Until the smoking ban, we didn't know how long this bar really was."

Union Square was just a couple blocks away. The W Hotel; a hip take on a coffee shop called Coffee Shop; and several other trendy and sparkling attractions beckoned the disposable income of a hip nightlife crowd. Old Town Bar, it seemed, was an accessible diversion to those places—a place less shiny that shiny people could visit to prove to other shiny people they did not have to be so shiny all the time. But the mice, he thought, made this place just the right amount of uncomfortable, and he loved it.

He finished his coffee. He became caught up in watching the very few patrons in the bar read their papers, talk about the Knicks or the Rangers, and enjoy afternoon snacks. He made a couple efforts to engage in his magazines. He, though, had lost his enthusiasm. He ordered a Captain and Coke. The soda's sugar would allow him to drink in the afternoon more efficiently.

Steve Martin's journal had been in his care now for about twenty-eight hours, and it occurred to him that he had not actually snooped through it like many would have. As a Steve Martin fan, this surprised him. He had turned a few pages and had gathered some proof of its ownership. But he had not read a word that would provide insight about Steve Martin.

He pulled the journal from his coat pocket and placed it on the bar. The book itself was quite unassuming: The size was about three-inches wide by five-inches tall. The cover was a nondescript brown, heavy paper that was only just lighter than cardstock. It was soft to the touch, as though it had been weathered by design. The cover's upper- and lower-right corners were rounded. The lower-left corner had been creased, as if at one time it had been folded over. From a distance its texture resembled that of a plain, brown-paper bag. Its pages were white with light gray rules. The writing within was in pencil, red ink, black ink and blue ink. There were no eraser marks, but many cross-outs and scribbles. The book was held together by a saddle stitch down the spine. The stitching was made of something more than thread and less than string. It was soft.

Navin stared at it as it sat on the bar, then picked it up and half-heartedly flipped through the book again. The same landmarks were clear: names, digits that appeared to be telephone numbers, other innocuous scribbles. Nothing held his interest, so he closed the book and promptly placed it back in his coat pocket.

"This is none of my business," he said under his breath. "Why am I not interested?"

His eyes grew empty. "Anyone would read this thing," he thought. "Anyone. Why not me? I'm a fan. My name is Navin R. Johnson, for shit's sake. What's wrong with me that I am not compelled to look at this thing?"

The internal chat that kept him occupied fragmented into unmemorable pieces as the bartender asked if he'd like another one, and then another, and then maybe just one more.

An encroaching fire truck's siren screamed and pulled Navin from a haze only he could see. Just as suddenly as he had noticed it coming, the truck arrived and sprayed Old Town Bar's inside with flashes of vivid red. As it passed, the Doppler Effect skewed and melted the siren's pitch until it faded into the echoing canyons of the city. He turned to look and realized that the truck's lights were made more brilliant by the darkness outside. He had drunk himself past dusk. "That's why I am thinking like this," he said. "I've had six drinks."

He sighed and paused, leaned to his left and reached into his right front pocket for his wallet. He paid his tab and, thinking he needed a dose of his newly found scripture, he checked the time:

5:37 p.m.

"Damn universe," he said. "Only does it when I need it to, not when I want it to."

He pushed through Old Town Bar's front door and

turned left toward a frantic Lexington Avenue. He hailed a taxi to return him to the Marriott. Once there, he thought, he would rest a bit, check some email and perhaps outlive his tipsiness. He would be ready for his steak in the green-and-white building.

Navin returned to Room 612 to discover his sobriety was actually intact. He threw his coat to the armchair near the window, kicked off his shoes and opened his laptop to check his email. Five emails were selling cleverly misspelled erectile dysfunction remedies at amazing discounts. There were three more offering a solution for short penises. There was one from South America that requested help in claiming twenty-one-point-five-million dollars. Its sender promised that if Navin sent a voided check, an eight-percent cut would be wired into his checking account. Then there was an email from Sid's Blackberry:

04:04 Sid Smalls
Navin. There's a lot in here that is pretty damning to her personality. I tried to see if I could take her side and see her perspective but damn it navin: steve martin?

ANIMAL RESCUE | 6

SID WAS LACONIC. ". . . damn it navin: steve martin?" was all he needed to write to put a redeeming smile on Navin's face.

"What were you doing wasting your time with someone who did not get Steve Martin?" Navin asked aloud. Sid had quickly found an obvious tear in the sail.

Sid's wisdom came from a deeply painful place, and a redemption that followed. It was a place created from events about which Navin knew, but dared not ask. It was marked by the lines in his face and the gray in his hair. But mostly, Sid's eyes were peaceful. Navin knew Sid had conquered something within. Even in an email response, Navin saw those wrinkles, and that gray, and Sid's placid gaze between the lines of a ten-point Courier typeface.

Navin wondered if Sid had identified Steve Martin as a litmus test for dating. Perhaps those truly familiar with Steve Martin shared a respect and admiration for him as a funny, emotive intellectual, and so they shared fundamental qualities that were not only desired for compatibility, but necessary. Thanks to Sid's reply, Navin wondered if he could ever be with anyone whose answer to the question, "Do you like Steve Martin?" was either, "Oh, he's alright, I guess," or "Wasn't he the old guy in 'Father of the Bride'?" The prospect that Steve Martin might be the filter through which all heartache in future relationships would be stopped, and all joy would be allowed to pass, intrigued Navin.

He reread Sid's response and noticed that it had landed in his inbox at 04:04. The time of the email was one thing. But of greater significance was that Sid took the time to read his very long vent. The Steve Martin reference was buried deep within his correspondence to Sid earlier in the day. That Sid had alluded to the reference made Navin feel as though he had listened to him, and it felt in so many ways like the first time anyone had in a decade. He felt far less alone. Looking forward to Sid's impending visit to Florida, he smiled widely.

In his exuberance, he scrolled down to read the entire exchange. He wanted to relive the experience of this dialogue with his friend. He noticed the time of his original email to Sid was 9:09. His faith in something, the identity of which still remained elusive, took a giant leap forward. Somehow through digital displays of time, he felt an invisible, benevolent presence embrace him.

He was not ready for the world to strip away this feeling. He quietly relished the smallest victories by sitting on the bed within the safety of his room. A door, a hallway, an elevator ride, a lobby and a sidewalk protected him from a world that could shove him back with one gust of subfreezing wind. These things would certainly be unable to keep the world out. But he was only trying to stay in.

Over the next hour, he peered aimlessly around his room. A detail on a section of wallpaper or a stain on the carpet often caught his attention. For the most part, however, he had reached a state he described as suspended animation. He was very much in the present. There was no temperature. If he were breathing, he didn't notice. His mind was blank. There was no past to rue and no future to fear. In this moment, he knew he wouldn't self-destruct. He couldn't self-destruct. The happiness he felt from a simple reply from a far-too-distant friend erased any form, function or thought. In a rare instance, he was enjoying a moment as he was in it, genuinely and effortlessly.

He slowly awoke from his peace to notice the evening slipping away. His plan to have a steak served by a man in a suit seemed shallow now, even contrived. He thought in-room dining would be more apropos. He looked at the menu and called room service. He ordered a ham and turkey wrap and two glasses of iced tea.

He returned to his computer to engage in the stream of consciousness that was surfing the World Wide Web. He checked his email and saw that someone on one of the online dating services to which he subscribed had e-flirted. FlaDiva had emailed him. Her photo was model perfect:

You look interesting and hot! Let's chat!!!

Alarm bells sounded. "Who," he asked, "throws 'hot' out there in an introduction?" Though he couldn't see the pool, he sensed diving into a shallow one could cause a head injury, so he responded with a test:

FlaDiva: Thanks for the compliments. Usually when someone uses two words to describe me they make no sense. Once I was told I seemed 'concave and wobbly' while another time 'plaid and porous.' So, thank you. Let's chat soon!

He would never get a reply.

There was no other mail, and so he logged on to one of the sites and aimlessly perused profiles of potential dates.

Skimming online dating profiles was a diversion that made him feel as though he was doing something—anything—social, but it was a game he reluctantly played. It shared many similarities to being picked last for a basketball team at schoolyard pick-up games. The nuance that escaped many grade-school kids is that not only were they picked last for their team, they were picked last for the *worst* team. The captain that picked them, after all, was the worst captain of the two by virtue of whatever decided the picking order. In an entire universe of possibilities, they were only chosen because there were no other choices. It mattered little if they could lead the yard in assists, could anticipate a pass or a shot, or had amazing stamina. It was largely an exercise in negative scouting that could cost a team a chance at victory. A stupid, careless remark three weeks before about getting an erection when Sister Mary Holywater walked into the classroom could cost a passable player the honor of being the *worst* player on the *best* team—or, at the very least, most popular team—for an entire semester. The schoolyard was *that* unforgiving.

Beyond this, he had also quickly realized that online dating was like anything else: No matter how honorable the premise, the integrity of any endeavor will sink to its lowest common denominator. Online dating will only be as good or as bad as its clientele, just as the fastest sloop in the world will only be as quick as its crew's abilities will allow.

Further, it was, in fact, degrading to a point. Navin likened it to selecting a pet to rescue from a shelter. It occurred to him that, therefore, online dating should borrow some of the process required to adopt a dog.

First, he thought, volunteers should handle each guy's marketing and profile. Volunteers, rather than paid professionals, make all the difference. It's hard to fire a volunteer. They are able provide an honest, anonymous opinion. These volunteers take one slapdash photo of each guy. Only one. This would prevent the guy from taking off his shirt or posting five hundred self-portraits, trying to look as seductive as possible.

Each guy had to be photographed with a bandana around his neck. The distraction caused by the bandana would equalize the playing field. Who looks good in a bandana? Aside from Willie Nelson, no one. This photo would be placed on a website.

Each photo would be identified with a fake name. So, John, Robert and Ted would be identified as Sparky, Gypsy and Bailey. After all, he thought, would a Ferrari be as attractive if it was known as a Pansy Violet?

Also, volunteers would write a very brief bio for each guy that prevents him, as well, from doing it himself. This eliminates phrases like "looking for my soul mate" and "I like romantic comedies." Both are phrases that mess it up for the rest of us, Navin thought, particularly those who *are* looking for their soul mates and *do* like romantic comedies. The descriptions would be limited to items like "better in a quiet, adult home," "good with children," "is recovering from abuse" and "has special needs, but with patient training can be housebroken."

All guys would be placed in kennels along a hallway

at the shelter. In this way job and career, as well as car and lifestyle, become nonfactors.

When potential adopters walk the hall, each guy will do his best to get her attention. Ninety percent will bark their heads off; bounce off the walls like lunatics; and a couple will actually pee themselves. These are the ones who are accustomed to getting anything they want and are really, really, *really* into sports.

Then there is always one who will eat his own poop, not ever truly realizing what's on the line.

Five percent will flash the saddest possible eyes. These are the manipulative ones—the ones most susceptible to infidelity.

Navin guessed women should look for the guy either sitting in the corner not amused with any of it, or happily playing with a chew toy. These guys are either retarded, grounded, deaf, independent, loyal, fun, or most of the above.

Should a woman spot a guy who sparks her interest, she asks for assistance and the guy is removed from his kennel and delivered to her in a waiting room. At this point, it gets really noisy. As her guy is walked down the hall, all the other guys go crazy—jumping, yelling with some howling, and others ramming their heads relentlessly against the kennel gates. The guys doing all the head-butting are the same who are really, really, *really* into sports.

As with selecting a dog from a pound, she should welcome the guy by ignoring him for five minutes. This will let her see if he is social. If he acknowledges her, then she should try to pet him behind the ears to see if he gets irritated. Finally, she should ask to feed him to check for food aggression.

At no time should he mouth her.

She should check for wounds, and remember a yawn is only a sign of nervousness and should not be taken personally. If he fails any of these tests, she should mark him off her list and have him returned to his kennel, which will instantly incite another riot amongst the others.

If he passes these tests, she should observe him once he is back in his kennel. If he doesn't brag to the others that he slept with her, she should consider adoption.

This, Navin thought, might increase integrity on these sites to an acceptable level.

In his quasi-partaking in online dating and networking sites, he had discovered two things: One, a generation of computer users had grown up with spell check and apparently refused to use it. Secondly, every girl wanted the exact same thing in a man:

> *I am a smart, sexy, sassy independent woman who wants someone to make me laugh, not try to change me, and knows how to treat a lady. I think a man with ambition, success with a hint of adventure is hot. My friends are soooo important to me, as is family. But if you can get me to laugh, we're half way there! :o) I am not looking for a relationship, but just email me and let's see where it goes!!! ;)*

A few more things struck him: First, he was apparently every girl's dream. *Every. Girl's. Dream.* He met all of these requirements. Funny? Navin. Not demanding? Navin again. Chivalrous, ambitious, successful? Navin, three times over.

Secondly, once he applied, he never got an interview. Either every guy fits every girl's wish list and the call back roster is unending; or looks do matter and perhaps he should remove his photo from the website. In either case, and at the very least, he thought he should get back a form letter:

Dear Applicant,

Thank you so much for your inquiry; however the position has been filled by another funny, chivalrous, ambitious and successful gentleman. Please visit this page again in the event the awarded party turns out to be lacking in any of those areas.

Sincerely,
Prty_jnk_n_da_trnk_94

Third, who *wouldn't* want all that? This really wasn't new information. So what's the point of any dating site giving anyone fifteen-hundred characters to write anything? They all write essentially the same thing. And since he had already established that spellchecking wasn't a priority, this certainly wasn't being used to exhibit intelligence or attention to detail.

He assumed every guy writes that he is all of these things on his page—funny, gentlemanly and successful. So, essentially, online dating was simply an online pick-up bar. There was really no difference. He could be ignored in either setting, and often was. At least online he didn't have to act as though he was checking text messages or was obliged to finish the drink he had just ordered before escaping. This epiphany caused him to rewrite his profile—partly out of rebellion for the online-dating scene, partly out of spite for Audrey and Jess, but mostly as an exercise to crack him up:

> *What I'm seeking: Ahem. One who doesn't get my jokes and finds them, and as a result me, exhausting. A plus if this person gets annoyed when I laugh at things she doesn't find funny. An inability to just appreciate me having fun is a must. I would like to rank someplace between 6th and 11th in priority behind career, mom and dad, friends, washing dishes, a puppy, yard work and water torture. Must be ungrateful if I choose to take her to some exotic getaway in a faraway land. I require someone who will take advantage of my big heart, never thank me for opening a door, and cause me to under-perform in my very successful career because I can't figure out how to make her happy. Unwillingness to pick up a dinner check—ever—a plus. She must be able to boast of me to her friends on girls' night out, and not be supportive of*

me when I am feeling down just hours later. Though not a deal breaker, if you have an irrational disdain for dryer sheets, can't follow driving directions or when drunk pass out in the middle of sex, email me today. Giving me startled, dirty looks in public a bonus. But careful, ladies: Over reactions to self-inflicted assumptions may prompt a marriage proposal! ;^) Must be self-aware enough to eventually call off our relationship out of love for me when she realizes she is unable to treat me well, yet maintain a level of self-absorption that will allow her to be self-righteously indignant as she does it. If you are all of these things, send me an unclear and ambiguous email full of things that, if I read them closely enough, I could figure out you have many wonderful qualities and I shouldn't be surprised when I discover them. My inbox is freaking loaded. Gotta run.

He found himself on his own page reviewing this artful and cryptic criticism of his recent relationship history and thought how angry this must sound to any woman who would read it. What he initially thought was funny any woman would quickly see as angry. In his current state of enjoying the present, he agreed. "Wow," he thought. "The clarity afforded when appreciating the present . . ." After a few moments scanning about his hotel room, he rewrote his profile:

> *I work hard to be very a good guy defined in a number of ways. Let's exchange a few emails and you can learn for yourself. Your code name is Marie Kimble.*

It had escaped his consciousness that he had just posted what may have been the world's first Steve Martin Online Relationship Compatibility Test.

༺༻

A tray lay on the hall floor outside Room 612, on which the remnants of Navin's dinner awaited collection by the Marriott's housekeeping staff. Late evening now, he rested in his bed satisfied from a quiet night of dining in and unremorseful for squandering his last night in New York City. Steve Martin's journal was out of sight, tucked inside his winter coat's breast pocket. He had spent the past couple hours flipping through hotel television channels and debating whether or not to masturbate while watching an in-room sex video. Most titles of these movies made him laugh. Often, they provided bemusement and admiration over and for whoever comes up with them. The current hotel selections included "Skank Wanks," "Suck-U-Lent Block Party VIII," and "What My Wife Won't Do."

Of course, once rented, these titles never appeared on the hotel bill. Navin's television promised that this method ensured his privacy and would prevent hotel personnel from judging him as they looked at his folio. But, as the only movies priced at sixteen dollars and ninety-nine cents, he knew that *they* knew exactly what was being rented. Nobody would rent "My Sister's Pussy, Cat" as a form of study for an impromptu oil painting, or in an effort to be caught up when "My Sister's Pussy, Cat II" was finally released. "Hitch," "The Wedding Crashers" and "Shrek the Third" would have appeared on the bill at seven dollars and ninety-nine cents, and he could not fathom anyone getting off to an animated ogre, even if it were voiced by Cameron Diaz.

He turned off the television and moved to his laptop, where non-formulaic entertainment awaited.

The Internet, he thought, was Chuck Barris' "The Gong Show" on performance-enhancing drugs. Online, he found an unscripted world. Each day, people so starved for attention would make asses of themselves on websites like YouTube. What once vilified Chuck Barris had turned into an industry that earned unimaginable fortune.

Faced with YouTube's search engine, he could think of nothing he wanted to see. Access to anything and everything at any time had frozen him. "Is this what it's like to have it all?" he asked himself. "When you can do anything, do you just choose not to?"

Completely unmotivated, he closed his laptop, went to the window for one final night view of a Manhattan intersection, then climbed back into bed. As he began to fade into tomorrow, he grinned at a faint and foggy vision of something better approaching. For much of the day, the clocks had told him so.

ೞ

The taxi slipped through the morning Manhattan rush hour, attempting to deliver Navin to LaGuardia Airport in time for his flight home. The sun was bright and the traffic was swift. Steam scrambled and scattered into the frigid air from seemingly every opening—car exhausts, manhole covers, people's mouths and noses and through scarves that hid them both. The taxi's pace was quick as it was leaving the city during an inbound rush hour.

Navin savored sightseeing—even after so many visits to New York City. He peered through passing coffee-shop, dry-cleaner and hair-salon windows to capture frozen portraits of New York City life: a man reading a paper while stirring his drink; a woman accepting a bag of soiled clothing from a well-dressed businessman; two women embracing as they prepare to receive the pampering they deserved in preparation for the event they were attending later in the evening. "Do they know," Navin thought, "their businessmen-husbands are cheating on them?"

He embraced these high-speed romps through the city, as they always provided a rapid slideshow of life inspiring art. They ignited his imagination. His scripting of the scenes he saw was automatic, and he would often feel empathy, joy or fear for whatever backstory he assigned to complete strangers.

His gaze was struck when his taxi driver swerved

suddenly to avoid a pedestrian who had thought she could beat a blinking don't-walk light. As a million car horns sounded, a muffled "fuck you" came from behind Navin's taxi. In the evasion, the cabbie had cut off a bicycle courier who was lane-splitting through slower traffic. The bike stayed upright on both wheels thanks to the reactions of an obviously skilled rider. Navin watched as the rider quickly caught up to his taxi and delivered a colossal spit ball that landed, accurately and purposefully, on the side window just in front of Navin's nose. He smiled broadly as the spit began to break apart and drift toward the rear of the moving sedan. "New York," he said fondly.

Over the Queensboro Bridge and into Queens, he passed through neighborhoods and by markets and endless structures adorned with marvelous graffiti. The taxi passed a public library whose marquee displayed, "Why not come in cool off and read a book or magazine?" He quickly surmised that the struggling marketing guru, who failed to make the library sound like a place anyone in this hard neighborhood might want to visit, must have died over four months ago, as it was now January and twenty-two degrees. The library's first selling point, the "cool off" part, had long since expired.

As LaGuardia came into view, he caught glimpses of a newer baseball stadium, taxi lines, bus queues and traffic cops. He was dropped near his airline, paid his cab fare and pulled his roller-board luggage into the terminal. The purgatory that was airport check in and security passed as painlessly as possible, to his appreciative surprise. Soon, he was in his requested window-coach seat and now a passenger on his journey home. Navin fell asleep before takeoff with his head rested against the window, as faint thoughts about the faint thoughts he had the night before fluttered aimlessly through his mind.

CINDY, ET AL | 7

"**DO YOU MIND** if we stop at a McDonald's and get a Quarter Pounder?" Geoff asked as he drove.

"Of course not," Navin said. He was still groggy from his midmorning nap aboard a Boeing 767. Navin wrestled within the confines of Geoff's coupe to shed his topcoat. The South Florida temperature was warmer by about fifty degrees than the subfreezing bitterness in New York. The sun was just as bright.

"I was wondering when you were going to take that thing off," Geoff said. Navin looked away, out the passenger's window into a sun-filled day. The drive wasn't anywhere near the cultural experience of a New York City taxi ride. The bounding cross-street intersections and masses of urban hikers were replaced by streets absent of sidewalks, but dotted with corner gas stations, fast-food restaurants, strip malls and the occasional bicycle rider.

"You just passed a McDonald's," Navin said.

"I know, I want to go to the one near my house," Geoff said.

"The new one?" Navin mumbled as he flexed his neck.

"Yeah. They owe me a buck seventy-nine," Geoff said rolling his eyes. "You've got to see this place; they haven't gotten an order right yet."

Navin grinned, but wasn't really interested.

"The other day, I stopped and ordered an Egg McMuffin and a large coffee, and they gave me a small coffee," Geoff said. He paused then asked, "Have you seen their small coffee?" It was the kind of are-you-listening-question with which he had baited Navin since they had met on a lawn at Mary Institute and St. Louis County Day School in 1981.

MICDS' roster of alum was as diverse as it was prestigious: Sara Teasdale and T.S Eliot. Dorothy Walker Bush and Senator John Danforth. Betty Grable and Vincent Price. Joe Buck and Shepherd Mead.

In 1980, the annual kindergarten tuition at MICDS could buy a new Datsun 210 Sedan, while tuition for grades five and higher would run one a brand new

Pontiac Firebird. But this esteemed education repelled Navin, and was simply dismissed by Geoff.

Geoff's father, James, gained the wealth required for a complete education worth the very home in which Geoff was raised by adapting flexible-shaft technology for use in plumbing snakes. Navin's father, Jerome, on the other hand, grew a small 1960's St. Louis appliance store into the region's Jerome Johnson's department-store empire. By 1972, he had amassed three St. Louis locations—one in Springfield, Missouri; two in Kansas City; and one each in Springfield and Peoria, Illinois. Jerome sold his stores to May Department Stores in 1975, left Doris alone with six-year-old Navin, and vanished. Jerome's parting gift to his son was enrollment into MICDS.

And so it was that a shit-digger's son and the son of an estranged Maytag dealer met and became friends amongst the ghosts of poets and authors, a matriarch of U.S. presidents and senators, World War II pin-up girls and horrorists, actors and sports commentators.

Jerome—to his credit, as Doris would explain—had not bought Navin an elite education. Jerome had secured for Navin a peer group. But, seeking escape from Jerome's gift Navin sought ingenuous summer jobs. He pumped gas at a Shell station just out of town. He worked in a traveling carnival. He once even applied to the United States Postal Service because, he thought, no one else he knew would. Years later he allowed himself a quirky moment of validation—he smiled upon learning that Andy Kaufman, at the height of his career, once secretly bussed tables at a diner.

It was his innate brilliance, however, that would subconsciously filter away the empty and the shallow, leaving just one, perhaps two, truly meaningful lifelong acquaintances.

And then there was Geoff.

Conversely, Geoff cared about just one thing at MICDS and that was Navin. Geoff seized upon Navin's reluctant acceptance of membership to the MICDS elite, and developed sophisticated ways that appealed to Navin's goodness and sensibilities. Geoff was able to horde Navin for himself and, for reasons truly unknown to Navin, he allowed it.

"Did you hear me?" Geoff asked. "Have you *seen* the size of their small coffee?"

"Yup," Navin said. "I heard you."

"So I told them I ordered a large coffee, and they charged me another seventy-nine cents, but my receipt showed I had paid for the large coffee at the first window."

"Mm-hmm."

"But I said, 'Fuck it,' and gave them the seventy-nine cents. It wasn't worth it. Then, the next morning, I ordered just a large coffee and the guy asked, 'How many creams?' and I said, 'Two.'"

"Mm-hmm."

"I get to the second window and they hand me two creams. They didn't even put them in for me. I'm driving, you know?"

"Uh-huh."

"Two mornings later, I order a large coffee on the way to work and it comes to $1.29. I give them two ones, a quarter and four pennies."

"Mm-hmm."

"The guy gives me back four quarters."

"Mm-hmm."

Geoff knew Navin was not interested by the way Navin hummed "Mm-hmm" after roughly every second pause in Geoff's tale.

Soon, they reached the McDonald's near Geoff's home and Geoff ordered a Number 4 meal with a large Coke. Geoff paid, and upon receiving the correct change at the first window said, "You owe me a dollar." Before the befuddled teenage Cuban girl could ask for details, he coasted to the second window. Once there, a different girl handed him a Number 4 with a large Coke.

"Must be a first-shift thing," Navin said. "And I thought they owed you a dollar seventy-something?"

"Seventy-nine," Geoff said. Geoff pulled from the drive-thru lane and asked Navin how his trip was as he snaked his hand through the McDonald's sack seeking to fill his palm with French fries.

"It was OK," Navin said. "Cold."

Geoff pulled into traffic, brought the car up to speed and took a sip of his Coke through a straw. "Have you heard from her?" he asked.

"Who?" Navin asked, fully knowing about whom he was asking, but wanting to act like he was over the whole thing.

"I guess . . . not," Geoff said. "Audrey."

"Oh," Navin said. "Of course. Uh, no, probably won't."

Navin winced at his error. By playing that he was not thinking about her, he had now made it impossible to have a conversation about her. A conversation about her would have been neither therapeutic nor cathartic. It wasn't even welcome. A conversation about her would have been, most honestly, something to talk about to keep Geoff from talking about Cindy. A dialogue about

Audrey would have prevented the inevitable, and perhaps gotten Geoff out of his head. He would immediately regret his inability to whine at the most needed of times. His chance for a preemptive strike had passed.

"Cindy didn't call this week, either," Geoff said.

Geoff was a tall, gangly man with beady eyes, a hump in his nose and a pointy chin. His lips were thin, and when he smiled one could see that his upper teeth angled back into his mouth. After just forty-four years, most of his hair had fallen out. He coated what remained with gel and spiked it upward. When shaving, he often missed a spot. It was not unusual for one to see some stray whiskers around the corner of his mouth. The next day they would be gone, while new whiskers appeared in a thin strip under his jaw line.

Geoff shuffled when he walked. And when he concentrated on anything—driving, walking, reading, thinking—Geoff's neck extended forward like a giraffe and his chin angled upward.

His nose always dripped. The center console in his car held a pile of balled tissues. In any situation, in any company, Geoff would pull a ragged tissue from his pocket and stick a pointed portion up his nose to intercept a trickle. Navin never shook his hand, as he could never remember a time when Geoff washed them.

Geoff wore foul-smelling cologne. In even finer restaurants, one could see him stick his finger in his ear and shake his hand from the wrist to alleviate the tickling itch deep within his ear canal. He sneezed loudly and the sneezes, combined with his breath, often smelled bad. His reasonably flat tummy matched his unreasonably thin arms and legs. His clothes were too large for him and hung as sheets on a clothes line from his shoulders and around his waist.

Years of listening to Geoff pine led Navin to believe that Geoff did not have the ballast required to prevent him from capsizing from the unsettled weights of his desires and fears. Now, as Geoff's dinghy would tip dangerously to one side, Geoff would lean heavily to counter it with the only balance he knew: his contrived desire to become a competent facilitator. He subconsciously bribed the world to accept him, and this kept him upright.

Whenever asked for anything, and whether he thought he could deliver or not, his answer was always, "Yes." He would deliver because he said he would. No one, including Navin, seemed to know how. In actuality, Geoff was a brilliant tradesman. His client list at the bank where he worked as a mortgage lender included many professions. He created relationships amongst his clients, and was always able to barter goods and services from the economic marketplace that was Geoff's Rolodex. And, because he always delivered on a promise, he got anything he asked for from anyone.

Navin wondered how Geoff was always available. How did he always have time to pick him up from the airport or waste a Wednesday afternoon away in some café? He assumed Geoff had used personal days, but he knew if he asked, Geoff would simply say, "It was a slow day."

Geoff was a dealmaker for everyone. Absent a personality, mainstream looks, healthy self-esteem or general happiness, his currency for a multitude of acquaintances was made from every other personal resource he had at his disposal. Short of love, a wife, a family, a pet, or a meaningful career, he turned pleasing others into his personal destiny and, therefore, his source of happiness.

This compensatory desire and need to please others, sadly, placed him in the precarious vulnerability of relentless and repeated heartbreak. His accomplishments in doing nice things for a woman he fancied, combined with her genuine appreciation for the deed, led him to misinterpret the signals. He bloated all gestures of gratitude to signs of affection. He kept a mental record of each and stuck it onto a tiny colored square around a mental Rubik's Cube. Once he became vainly infatuated with anyone, he would turn and twist his cube in endless hopes that once solved, it would reveal his happily ever after. Or, at least a game plan toward it.

He was so consumed with helping people that he had never noticed that no one had ever done anything nice for him first. As he always received gratitude because he gave a woman reason to be grateful, he never received care because he never gave a woman a reason to be attentive. Nor did he give her the chance. He always struck first because he never believed anything would be offered.

Cindy was preceded by Cynde, who was preceded by Sin, who was preceded by Cindee, who was, fittingly, preceded by Cindy. Every girl on whom he developed a crush over the past two years was named some derivative of "Cindy." That each Cindy was attractive, smart, funny, charming and a phenomenally great human being lead Navin to believe that Palm Beach County, Florida must have the largest number of Great-People-Named-A-Derivative-of-Cindy per capita in the world.

Navin referred to the collective whole of Geoff's lack of a love life as The Cindies: "What are we going to do about the Cindies?" meant, "How are we going to get Geoff into a relationship?" or, "We must get Geoff laid."

As people, the real individual Cindies were women who adored Geoff, but just not enough. Each Cindy genuinely cared for him and was grateful for the value he added to her life. Geoff would become her best friend because he was easy to talk to. Like Navin, he was a great consult. Eventually, as the friendship would grow, a Cindy would finally ask him to advise her on how to handle her own love life, or worse yet, a specific man whom she would like to have for her own.

Navin watched as the scenario repeated without end. Geoff eventually met each Cindy's suitor over drinks or dinner, and watched a more attractive man charm and slither his way into Cindy's panties. He would watch the seduction of Cindy unfold before his eyes in excruciatingly slow motion. The most ostentatious suitors were particularly bothersome. His infatuation with a Cindy was confounded with a desire to protect her from anyone he viewed as beneath her. Thanks to the pedestal on which he placed her, no man was worthy. Except, Geoff hoped, for him.

His affections for a Cindy employed the curse that was his delusion. These fantasies were scripted by him and inspired by her. There were times that Navin feared Geoff actually believed he was on his way—or already in—a relationship with a Cindy.

Inevitably, another man would take the role Geoff had written for himself. Like a sixth sense, he always seemed to know when a Cindy and her new man had surrendered to their passions. Navin's hunches were confirmed when Geoff would appear to him, often very early in the morning.

Over the years, Navin grew exhausted of Geoff's choice to stay near a Cindy as her best friend and thus assume a front-row seat to the revealing of her happiness. Though Geoff never told him, Navin knew Geoff was hopeful that he would be there when she fell and she might see his real value to her as something more.

Navin dutifully served as a sounding board to Geoff's intense grief, but it never lasted long. Navin reckoned it was because Geoff had actually grieved the entire time he knew a Cindy: Geoff would wait and desperately hope for her to make a move or start a conversation. She wouldn't, and before bed he dropped a coin into his pity jar. The coins summed to a significant prepayment, and so finality was quick once he decided to move on. "When I was a kid, I used to imagine being at my parents' funerals," Geoff once told Navin. "That way, when they actually died, I would be ready for it." He had applied the same technique in his adult life for all bad things he thought were inescapable.

Navin was sad for Geoff, as he felt he framed his desire—Navin never called Geoff's feelings for them as love—as friendship, and so he never invited them to explore him as anything more.

"Cindy didn't call you at all?" Navin asked.

"No," Geoff said. "I know she was with Bart in the Keys this weekend, so I'm sure she was busy."

Of course she was busy, Navin thought. She was getting her brains balled out by a guy named Bart. This is what he needed to say to Geoff, but didn't have the heart. The timing wasn't right, he reasoned, but when would it be? Geoff never took time off from his crushes long enough for Navin to lay it on the line. The great trapeze act, The Flying Cindinies, was always in midair. It would be like trying to have a conversation while skydiving.

"She's got a lot going on right now," Navin said gently. "A new relationship, it's going well. Your friendship with her will be different now."

"I know," Geoff said, holding his half-eaten Quarter Pounder with his left hand while his right hand guided the steering wheel.

"Where's the extra dollar?" Navin quickly asked hoping to change the topic.

"What extra dollar?" Geoff asked.

"McDonald's . . ."

"Oh, yeah, yeah, yeah . . .," Geoff sparked. "I gave the same girl that ripped me off from the seventy-nine cents a ten and a one and some exact change for a check that came to just over six bucks and some change, and she gave me back five ones, which defeated the purpose of me giving her the extra single in the first place because I wanted a fiver, but when I got to the second window, I counted the ones and she had only given me four singles, so at the first window I thought she was dumb, and then at the second window I thought she was incompetent, and you want to know the worst part?"

"Worst part?" Navin whispered.

"The next day, I gave her a ten for a check that was under five dollars and she gave me back a twenty," Geoff said, now clearly getting worked up. "So I told her that she gave me too much change, and she reluctantly took the twenty back and gave me the correct amount. And when I drove to the second window, I saw her being hugged and consoled next to the French-fry fryer by the manager and surrounded by three or four other employees, and one was rubbing her back . . . and they all turned at once to look at me as if I had raped her cat."

"And they still owe you a dollar?" Navin provoked.

"One-seventy-nine," Geoff corrected. "But, 'You owe me a dollar-seventy-nine' doesn't roll off the tongue so well in a drive-by verbal assault, so I just say a dollar."

"I see your point," Navin conceded. "Hey," he said with a sparkle in his eye. "I have great news!"

"What's that?"

"I met a girl on the plane and she lives here. I gave her your number. Her name is Cindy."

"Grrrf," Geoff moaned.

❦

Navin threw his travel bags toward the closet door near his bathroom, where they would remain unpacked until he had reached a time when doing laundry was absolutely necessary. He cleared the pockets of his overcoat and pants and placed the most critical items—his wallet, phone and Steve Martin's journal—on the end table next to his bed. He slung his coat toward the closet, where it hung about three-hundred-thirty days of the year.

It was now mid-afternoon, and the peace with which Navin left New York just that morning was largely displaced by the continuing saga of Geoff and the Cindies. He held a great deal of empathy for Geoff. But listening to Geoff's recurring disappointments over the Cindies, and now his displacement of the anger toward the neighborhood McDonald's, gave Navin perspective on his own life. He could clearly classify his own recurring misery as the product of bad luck, bad timing or bad choices. The frustration of Geoff and the Cindies lay in the premise that Geoff's hopelessness was self-inflicted. Navin always felt he gave his best effort. The cause of his frustration was far more unsatisfying than Geoff's, as it devalued his identity. Why were Navin's best times lost to him? Why did someone else own them? Why did he allow that? And, finally, when would he find the one who would be there to walk down a boulevard richly adorned with epic happiness?

Though those questions didn't flow as succinctly or as clearly in his mind as he wanted, they were there and he did have his fingertips upon them. His impatience was becoming his true nemesis.

He wasted the day and scrolled through his TiVo playlist for anything interesting to watch on television. The list contained first-run relics from an already-run relationship: The TiVo had largely been programmed by Audrey. "I don't even like TV," he said aloud, then pointed the remote control to the television and turned it off.

A frozen pizza and two hours of surfing the Web lead him to prepare for bed. He brushed his teeth, rinsed, wiped his lips dry and dropped the towel to the sink. He braced himself palms down on the vanity and peered into his eyes. "Maybe tomorrow," he said.

Once he had settled in bed, his quiet apartment amplified a barrage of incomplete thoughts and fantasies. He could not complete a single thought. He could not fantasize about a desire before his imagination rerouted the premise into something totally unrelated. Frustrated with his wandering mind, Navin glanced to the end table to see Steve Martin's journal. Despite his vow not to snoop into Steve Martin's personal life, he reached over and pulled the diary to his hip and began to flip through it.

The journal contained a number of cryptic notes that seemed to be categorized in some way. Quite a few pages were labeled by the names of films, a stage play and books—"The Spanish Prisoner," "Picasso at the Lapin Agile," "The Pleasure of My Company." Under these headings were scribbles that looked like production notes. The book contained the names of actors, directors, venues and locations. There were some orphaned phone numbers, and those numbers that were not orphaned were referenced only by initials. Navin thought it odd that so many pages of Steve Martin's journal were dedicated to reference materials.

Few were the interesting pages. These contained a few short, cryptic thoughts that formed no complete idea whatsoever:

Blond Hair, Blind Dog, Bland Potatoes
Dearest Family, and Steve . . .
Diamonds are forever, but corn is for lunch.
Why do I have to do all the pining?

He simply skimmed the journal before asserting that this was nothing of his concern. With disappointment, he deemed Steve Martin's journal to have no entertainment value. "At least there could be a Sudoku puzzle in there," he thought. His eyelids grew heavy, and his eyes stung from fatigue. He began to think he should simply return the journal to Steve Martin. He intended just one last flip through the pages, when as he did three written lines leapt from an unassuming page to command his attention:

Eh! Star like charmer hated porno.
If wrong be, I am wanted and deplored.
The warm town inhabits, earns TV time.

He read it a second time, and then a third. At best, it was a verse of poetry. At the very least, intriguing jabberwocky. "Shakespeare?" he asked. "But with references to pornography and television?"

In a journal that, upon the most cursory of glances was devoid of literary art or comedic value, this verse had an artistic intrigue that was absent elsewhere within the notebook.

His excitement at finding something that might be enlightening lost out to his demanding fatigue for his attention. And so, in a single motion, Navin dropped the journal onto his end table and pulled the chain that delivered darkness to his room. Rolled onto his side and with a pillow tucked beneath his arm, he loosely pondered the verse's significance. Having something now that held his attention until he fell asleep, he faded peacefully with the hint of a grin upon his face.

☙

Navin's eyes snapped open and, after quickly gathering himself, he glanced to the clock to see it was 2:15 in the morning. Within a moment, something heavy was pressing down.

The dream from which he had just awoken was unclear. His mind was a fog and he felt insecure. Something terminal was about to happen to him.

He rolled to his left into a fetal position and clutched a pillow. "Get back to sleep," he said. "Let this feeling pass." But he thought that sleep was impossible. He had made sleeping a vital objective. He had thought about it. It would now be difficult.

Navin's heart began to race. The loneliness deep within had manifested into an imperceptible dream. Now awake, he knew he was in danger. He could not open his eyes to break the steady stream of flashes from his previous relationships. With each passing second, the hair on his body arose as if the static attraction of a very slow and very deliberate, a very metaphoric yet very real, a very fragile yet very determined ceiling was pressing down and nearing his body from above.

Navin had never felt such fear in any circumstance, real or imagined. This was real. Death would now be a relief, but not before the horrifying panic that precedes the drowning of those who are trapped beneath a sheet of ice with no way to the very air they can see but not taste.

Navin tried to physically roll to his right to escape the falling sky. His torso's girth, however, was too wide to allow his passage beneath this demon's boot. He then wiggled and slid to his left, but the oppressing force had no end. "This is not real!" he said aloud. "This is not real. This is a new day." He knew this was within his control, yet seemed powerless to do anything about it.

For a moment, the sky opened and the pressure was gone, only to return and pick up where it had left off the instant he closed his eyes. Navin was about to be crushed by his thoughts and emotions.

His bottled-up feelings of hopelessness, loneliness and a lifetime of botched opportunities for happiness had caught up. Here on this mattress—his only refuge from the world, his security blanket for his entire adult life, the only thing that had not disappeared—he would die on the whim of his subconscious.

Of all this he was acutely aware, but he could not change the sensations he felt. He was not asleep and this was not a dream. He was very much awake and alert. His pep talks were brief, regurgitated passages from books he had read. But for each Winston Churchill quote, there was an all too vivid memory of a happier time, or happiest time, with someone who didn't exist anymore.

A proud smile from across the crowded room. Discovering Juliet's balcony in Verona. Dancing at The Quays Pub in Galway. A fifteen-year-old bottle of Brunello di Montalcino on a Venice canal. Getting high at Coffeeshop Picasso in Amsterdam. The adventure of a broken-down train in the Austrian Alps.

Each memory brought Navin closer to suffocation. Emotion pressed against the back of his eyes as if gallons of tears were seeking escape but could not find a pinhole through which to do so. His stomach tightened and his jaw clenched. His fist clutched the nearest loose pillowcase. He felt the ceiling begin to press against his upward most shoulder now. His eyes squinted tightly and a scream formed in the back of his throat, but would not come. He pressed his knees to his chest to curl up in a most defensive position.

"I'm having a panic attack," he said, not really

knowing if he was while desperately seeking an escape from his own mind. With that, Navin grabbed his pillows, sprung from his bed and ran from the bedroom that now seemed to house all his demons.

Across the hallway on his living room sofa, he found his new refuge where he immediately fell asleep without a further dream that he would recall or fear. It was over, and when he awoke he held a vague memory of the terror that consumed him just hours before.

TRANSLATION 8

WHILE EATING FRUIT Loops from a bowl, Navin peered through his front-door window, past the corner of the adjacent home, to get a morning glimpse of the Atlantic Ocean. His apartment, located just two blocks north of Palm Beach's famed Worth Avenue, occupied the top floor of a two-story house that was just three narrow properties from the beach.

With this locale, a monthly rent of twenty-four-hundred dollars was a steal. Navin saw past the marketing pundit's claim of "old-world charm" when he signed the lease four years before. To him it only meant that the abode badly needed a level floor, new plaster, fresh paint, new appliances, a dishwasher and the replacement of a rusting cast-iron bathtub. He was reluctant to take a bath for fear that once full of water he and the weighted tub would crash through the floor and flatten the dog that lived below. On one hand, he liked the idea of the dog's demise. It was an unattended, baying nuisance. On the other hand, being collected by the coroner while wet and naked amongst jagged pieces of a broken bathtub and dog seemed undignified.

Stairs that clung to the home's east face provided the only access to his apartment. His path from door to car was exposed to any ocean weather that attacked the coastline from the east. Wind made the metal staircase seem rickety at best, though Navin believed that the steps' movement below his feet during stormy times was a figment of his paranoia. Certainly if he were to perish in or around his home, he thought, his death would be caused by bathing.

Navin's income afforded a choice of living arrangements: Purchase a very nice home inland, or rent the small four-room apartment near the surf, beach and in the midst of high society. Building equity in a home, he thought, meant nothing if he were bartering quality of life. And a home on the sea—and on the Island of Palm Beach, nonetheless—was certainly a significant contribution to his lifestyle.

As he dredged the bowl for the remaining teaspoons

of pinkened milk, he became increasingly unsettled. Though unclear, a memory of his midnight panic attack was in there, somewhere. The sun was bright, the surf was emerald green, and in the streets the beachgoers hadn't a care. But this was the present, and he was stuck someplace between enchanting-but-useless memories of the past and the fear of never experiencing any of them again. Navin was beginning to understand that as the devaluing of these memories was eating him away, they were proof that he had done his best to find happiness with another. Somehow, his best wasn't enough. He was far too self-centered to get the bird's-eye view. He could only bemoan that bird shit, like his self-esteem, obeys the law of gravity. He was beneath each.

Navin turned from the door to wash his bowl and placed it in the cabinet. With each step over an area rug and through his living area to the kitchen, his mood saddened. His bowl clanked as it nested into a stack of other identical bowls, and his spoon landed on its side in the fork compartment of a rubberized flatware organizer. After a pause, he noticed that the microwave oven's digital clock stated the time as 8:08. *Faith is the answer to peace of mind.* The universe, he thought, bore witness to his panic attack. "Thanks for noticing," he said to his microwave and turned away. To an empty kitchen, the oven displayed YRWLCM.

Smiling now, Navin recalled the verse he had spotted within the pages of Steve Martin's journal. This was interesting to him, not because he felt the verse held the key to the universe or any great unknown insight into Steve Martin, but because it felt like the beginning of a creative process.

He excelled in the process of creating a product—its branding, packaging and marketing. Turning an idea into a publicly demanded property is what he did with restaurants, nightclubs and, much earlier in his career, a fishing pole that could fit into one's pocket.

Navin often snickered that it was only after people paid nineteen dollars and ninety-nine cents and got two collapsible fishing poles for the price of one, they still had to deal with carrying live worms or crickets. Further, if the fishing rod worked, they had to find a way to get the fish they had caught home.

He was fascinated in how comics, acclaimed speakers and authors were essentially single-proprietorship corporations. They conducted their own research and development, as well as packaging and marketing. He truly appreciated how painfully lonely the process could be. Therefore, the diligence required must be borne from a place misunderstood by most.

Great artists, Navin reconciled, were talented. But successful artists, he extrapolated, were brilliant entrepreneurs.

There was plenty of room, he thought, in and around art for commercialism. Those artists who bucked any potential capitalism simply didn't possess the skillsets to market their life's passions. These artists ultimately betrayed their own talents by truncating their audience.

The verse within the pages of Steve Martin's journal was a seed and it led, or would lead, to something artistic. With Steve Martin's journal in hand, Navin returned to his living room and sank into his sofa. He opened the book to the verse to contemplate its destiny:

> *Eh! Star like charmer hated porno.*
> *If wrong be, I am wanted and deplored.*
> *The warm town inhabits, earns TV time.*

Navin quickly reasoned the obvious: *Eh! Star like charmer.* The protagonist was likable and had a certain charisma. He obviously viewed himself as virtuous, however defined, as the first line of the prose clearly identified his disdain for pornography. But, what man disliked pornography? Republican men? Would Steve Martin make the protagonist of his latest opus one that held conservative values? "Unless he was a she," he thought.

Or was "porno" a metaphor for anything less than acceptable in the mainstream? Or was "porno" symbolic of anything devoid of artistic value? In this case, the protagonist would be more liberally inclined.

Either conservative or liberal, man or woman, this person needed a name, and so Navin assigned the names "Bill" for a male and "Alice" for a female.

At first blush, the second line seemed equally as obvious: *If wrong be, I am wanted and deplored.* Pornography or art, or lack thereof, could not easily be categorized as "right," "wrong," "good" or "evil." It was a matter of free will to the participants and observers. The pursuit victimized no one as long as the opinions or the act only involved the willing. But, regardless of Bill or Alice's position on pornography, they would be wrong to half the people, most assuredly, all the time. Therefore, each side would have equal energized levels of acceptance or rejection. Either way, Bill or Alice will be popular or reviled.

The third line indicated to Navin there would be

controversy: *The warm town inhabits, earns TV time.* The town, a naïve or innocent community, would become the place for a conflict over Bill or Alice's actions. Attention would be drawn, obviously, by way of television. He envisioned a climax that involved satellite trucks and news helicopters that besieged a typically sleepy town. This made sense to him, because from great chaos can come great comedy. According to the verse, chaos was inevitable.

The word "if" in the second line, he noted, foretold of something heavier than a simple opinion. It created conflict. It told him Bill or Alice was unsure of their position on an issue, the actions they would take, and what consequences may lie ahead. He was sure, though, that Bill or Alice was following their heart and that, quite likely, they had little else on which to go.

"A crisis in faith," he declared aloud. "Head-versus-heart causes chaos . . . in three lines. Brilliant."

☙

"So, you found Steve Martin's journal and you think the universe is communicating to you through it," Geoff said.

"I think so," Navin said. "Maybe."

"Really?"

"You're not buying it."

"Well, no, not really. What's the message, Navin? If you build it, they will come? Are you going to go build a baseball diamond in the middle of The Breakers' golf course?"

"No, nothing like that," Navin said. "Look, I've been getting signs. Some force, I think, is trying to wake me up. Maybe see things a little differently."

"Really, are you serious right now?"

Navin cringed. "Don't say that. Jess said that. It only exposed her stupidity. Anyway, I mean there is a conflict in Steve Martin's journal, or at least I'm treating it like one. It's exciting, actually. Head versus heart. It's speaking to me. Something else to fucking think about for a change. I want to figure it out."

The two fell silent as they ate their lunches beneath a perfect South Florida sky, and watched the boats pass on the choppy Intracoastal Waterway that divided West Palm Beach and Palm Beach.

"It's a moat," Geoff said.

"What?" Navin asked confused. "The verse in the journal is a moat?"

"The Intracoastal is a moat," Geoff said nodding to the waterway across Flagler Drive. "Keeps the bad people off the island," Geoff said.

"I see," Navin said. "That's what the Palm Beach Police Department does."

"No, they are there just in case the bad people make it across somehow. The moat does all the work."

"Are you suggesting it's manmade?"

"Of course not, but it has a purpose. Look, three blocks behind us the same one-hundred-ninety-five-pound, five-foot-three-inch hooker lifts her shirt and shows me her giant, sagging titties every morning as I drive to work and says, 'Hey, Hunnnn, how 'bout a taste?' She's not getting across *that* waterway."

"She'll get arrested," Navin said. "That's the deterrent."

"Yes, *if* she gets across that waterway," Geoff stressed. "You think the boat traffic is by accident? All these bridges are drawbridges. It's all synchronized. Once Thunder Box and others like her get within an eighth of a mile of the bridges, the boat traffic increases and the spans go up. Lose the hookers and drug dealers and you'll fix the traffic congestion."

Navin laughed at Geoff's conspiracy theory.

"Why are you laughing, Navin?" Geoff asked pointedly. "You believe so much in the human spirit that it is beyond the rich and powerful to build castles and seal themselves off from regular people? Lot of good that human spirit has fucking done you. You sleep alone at night now, don't you? You do your fucking best and you get your fucking—"

"Whoa, Geoff . . . I was just—" Navin said.

"Whoa, what?" Geoff snapped. He went back to poking through his salad with a fork. Navin looked up into a pure-blue heaven, drew a breath and looked down to watch a very attractive woman wrapped in pink spandex Rollerblade past him down Flagler.

"I'm sorry, Geoff," Navin said. "You're right. It's probably all by design."

And so it was at lunch that Navin began to realize that they had grown tired of each other's advice and encouragement. Geoff had begun to speak at him as he did the teenager at McDonald's.

It had used to be that when they tried to help each other, the advice was perfect and spot on. Neither, however, could apply the same wisdom to themselves. Navin watched as Geoff was becoming more cynical, more withdrawn and more unpleasant. The chip on his shoulder was becoming an entire block. With every new Cindy came a bigger grudge. He did not know where Geoff was headed, but knew he didn't want to go there.

"C'mon, Navin," Geoff said resuming his assault. "Steve Martin's journal is here to save your soul? You fucked up Jess. How could you fuck up Jess, Navin? You had what everybody wants, including me. And you didn't have the respect for the rest of us to *not* fuck it up. Fuck you, Navin. I don't feel badly for you. You let us all down. I feel badly for me." And with that Geoff sprung up, his chair squeaking along the floor, and left the restaurant.

"Jess?" Navin asked himself. He sat stunned and stung. While in shock, he initially gave credence to what Geoff had to say. In a flash, he questioned everything he believed to be true about all that happened with Jess. But a single flash later, he rose from the table and chased Geoff into the parking lot.

"Hey!" Navin yelled. "Hold on," he said jogging toward Geoff.

"What?" Geoff said without breaking stride.

"You're pissed because I try and you don't," Navin said.

Geoff stopped and turned to face Navin. "C'mon, that's ridiculous," Geoff barked.

"Get your own fucking Jess," Navin said. "Get your *own*."

"Fuck you! You get all these women and can't keep them because you are too goddamn into yourself," Geoff said. "It's insulting."

"To whom?" Navin asked. "Insulting to *you*?"

"Yeah, me!"

"Well, whether or not if I could have kept one, it wouldn't change the fact that you still would not have landed one single Cindy anyway. You'd still be sleeping alone, waiting for the world to hand-deliver your happiness."

Geoff's eyes watered and his posture fell. He pulled a balled tissue from his pocket and pressed it into his nostril.

This was the first time Navin had ever seen Geoff try to be this assertive, and he had just slapped him down. But Navin knew it had caused him to finally speak the truth, unreservedly.

"Look," Navin said, and looked around the parking lot. "Why did you give them the extra seventy-nine cents?"

"What?" Geoff asked.

"At McDonald's," Navin recalled. "You were right, you had a receipt, and you still gave them an extra seventy-nine cents."

"It's just a diversion."

"No, it's not just a diversion. The McDonald's saga is *not* just a funny anecdote. You think you are paying into some magic cosmic bank account that is keeping score. You're not pissed because you took it on the chin for some extra coin. You're pissed because you didn't act on what you knew."

"What's this got to do with anything?"

"Everything," Navin said. "You just show up and expect a payoff. And it doesn't come. And, worse yet, it goes in the other direction. They get your change wrong, and your order, and don't put fucking cream in your fucking coffee, and the Intracoastal Waterway was created by God to protect the elite, and I am just trying to get some stuff right, and *you're* offended."

Geoff looked to the ground and again wiped his nose. Navin was searching for a connection.

"You can't just show up, Geoff. You have to ask. You have to fucking try. Now you hang around the McDonald's like you hang around the Cindies, just hoping they'll get it right on their own: One day, a kid inside a McDonald's drive-thru window who can't even speak English is going to reach through and hand you two extra dollars while you get a hand job from a Cindy. But it won't happen, Geoff. You're too scared to ask, too scared to fail. I've got news for you: You're already failing, Geoff." Navin paused to allow Geoff to catch his breath. "You leave my shit out of it."

Geoff said nothing as Navin turned to reenter the restaurant and pay the check. He was sure he had hurt Geoff, probably quite badly. But he was also certain he spoke the truth, because it stung him to hear it himself. He realized that what he had said to Geoff applied, to a large extent, to him as well. "I guess that's why I knew the material so well," he thought.

The short drive over the Moat of Palm Beach to his apartment put Navin into a daze. His mind quickly scanned the archived emotions he had felt for Jess and Audrey. For the most part, he remembered being happy, comfortable and content. With Jess, he remembered being lazy and horny. With Audrey, he remembered being offended and inadequate. But with each, he refused to let go.

He was home soon. He had no desire to go inside. He sat on the second step of the staircase that led to his apartment's front door. He watched as dogs on leashes and children on bikes passed by his house going to and coming from the beach. Seagulls swarmed above, and a car alarm sounded from afar. His outburst toward Geoff moments before left him with a sad conclusion: He and Geoff were in the same place.

Both were guilty of confusing a feeling too commonly described as "love" for something that was only the opposite of being lonely. What they felt was a feeling that was one part companionship, one part appreciation, one part yearning and one part appetite. The feeling, however, was most certainly not love. It was the absence of love that drove each into profound sadness.

OBLIVION | 9

LATER IN THE evening, Navin caught up on the news. It had been about a week since he had left for New York, and the world had escaped his view. He went online and found the fresh news was the same as the stale news: In Afghanistan, yet more people met explosive deaths. In the United States, a congresswoman said something dumb. In Europe, a terrorist organization's sleeper cell had been busted; a historic church in Germany had burned; and eight tourists were killed in a train accident in Austria. He didn't read past the headlines. It was all the same. The real fresh news was always in the tabloids. He liked the rags. He found them absurd, and found it ludicrous that this was an actual industry. It made him feel that he was the smartest person reading them, even if he had to join *that* club to feel *that* way.

In entertainment news, a prolific Italian crooner of whom Navin had not heard had died from a brain hemorrhage. The hemorrhage was described as "unexpected."

A former child star from the network television sitcom "My Life Stinks Like Booty" was admitted to a rehab clinic, the very day her father was released from the same rehab clinic.

And "Bonzo," the former Hollywood item of actress Bonnie Jasper and Latin pop sensation Gonzo Chavez, was embroiled in a nasty custody battle involving Bonnie's three stepchildren from her previous marriage to legendary eighty-nine-year-old film director Milo Perzhucnitz. After allegations that Perzhucnitz lip-synched most of his directives on seven of his last ten films, he died unemployable and penniless while in exile somewhere on the Canary Islands. The stepchildren—Francis, Poots and Sherman—were fifty-two, forty-six and forty-five-and-a-half years of age, respectively. Two were married with children and the third, Francis, had just one arm. The story suggested that Poots' and Sherman's extended families, and Francis' special needs, would play in Bonnie's favor during the custody proceedings.

He also stumbled across the story of a sixty-eight-year-old gentleman who had awoken from a coma after eighteen years. His wife sat with him in his Budapest hospital room and read the news to him each day without fail. When he awoke, he only said "Köszönöm."

Navin searched online for the meaning of a word he could not pronounce, and found it to be an expression of thanks. He returned to hover on this story. It had nothing to do with him, really, nor his current situation. It was just a wonderful story, and it caused him to propound that "I love you" may not always be the most meaningful phrase in a relationship. An expression of gratitude, he thought, perhaps meant more.

His cursor floated across the screen and passed over a hot link that prompted a pop-up box:

COMA [ˈkō-mə] A state of deep, often prolonged unconsciousness, usually the result of injury, disease, or poison, in which an individual is incapable of sensing or responding to external stimuli and internal needs.

The Hungarians' sweet story fueled the epiphany that Navin had been asleep. There had been an unrevealed injury, disease or poison in his past that placed him into a coma. What was it? How long ago? He quickly resolved to not care what this event, or series of events, might have been. Of highest import was his coma's length, and at what point did he begin to awaken? The most substantive question was, as it pertained to his conflict and issues, yet resolved: When would he fully regain consciousness?

He could argue that he had been asleep his entire life. He never quite got things. He tended to be naïve. Despite an inherent cynicism, he saw the world through soft filters. All things were good even when they were not—as a child, a teen, a young adult, an adult, a companion, a lover and a friend.

Never a cliché were truer: Ignorance *was* bliss. For as long as he could remember, he had been unfulfilled, lacking in something someone else had, deficient in some required skill, and unsettled by some boogeyman he had locked in the cellar years before.

But he had the means to sweep it all away with a sense of humor, a practical logic and indulgence in the best of anything within his reach. For years with Suzy, and then with Jess and Audrey, he sought happiness by sharing the things he thought gave him joy. It was here in his thoughts Navin discovered another critical distinction: The same things that brought one person joy may just as effectively numb, as well. His disease was a chronic unhappiness, and his poison was escape. Years of applying various forms of this salve deepened his coma. By the time he and Suzy had broken it off, he was fully asleep and was unable to feel the true, life-fulfilling emotions for which he had longed and actually received with her. Like a punch-drunk fighter who wins by a split decision, Navin had won the fight, but could feel no joy. He only raised his arms because that is what one does after victory. He was just glad it was over.

Navin sleepwalked into Jess' life and mistook something new for something alive. She was a new sedative. Her desire to escape her own marriage and lonesomeness expedited her effect on him. No comfortable reality could awaken him from his soporific overdose. It was simply a matter of time before the world would wrangle away the comfort of one of them and replace it with a bed of nails. For whatever reason, Jess' awakening was sudden and shocking when Russell changed jobs. Navin's awakening only began when Jess left. The deeper the sleep the ruder the awakening, and as a small baby screams when startled from sleep, Navin's soul did, as well. He actually felt something and it scared him. It hurt him and confused him. Seeking recovery, this very bright and compassionate man peered at a blank canvas and eight tubes of paint and had no idea where to start. Beyond not knowing how to even hold a brush, he could not articulate his frustrations with what stood before him. He had been *that* asleep.

Thousands of digital clocks along the eastern seaboard had begun speaking to him. A Hungarian couple whose names he could not recall touched his heart. And Navin had kilned the first brick of understanding. He was able to look at a daunting mushroom cloud and simply ask, "What do I do now?"

☙

"Should I welcome this news so openly as to dismiss all that is inherently amiss with its premise?" Steve Martin asked beneath the bright-white spotlight that shone from someplace high above the theater's seats. "And, if I should, then shouldn't you be compelled or, at the very least, obliged to offer an explanation for my acceptance of all things unacceptable?"

"Oh please, sir, I beg of you," a mousy redheaded girl

delivered. "For this news is nothing new, it is very old. It begs for your attention, your wisdom, your compassion—"

"Enough!" snapped Steve. "Should I be so irresponsible to my soul, to my *very* soul, to my very *just* and *righteous* moral compass as to look the other way to this artless effort, this thing that evokes neither a genuine feeling of love, nor compassion, an item void of redeeming value?"

"But, sir, I—"

"Pornography! Utter *pornography*! You ask that I accept your offering as something other than pornography?"

"Pornography, sir, is in your interpretation, not in its genesis, if I may be so contrary."

"Being contrary, Miss Alice, is the least of your transgressions as the breach of the heart's sanctity truly— and I mean truly as spelled t-r-u-l-*E*-y—is repulsive."

"Please, Sir Bill, understand that though we may disagree on the result, the source of our disagreement is noble and just and, therefore, a united front between us will and shall transform the consequence you fear into the reward you seek."

"You must understand that Lady Cindy shall have none of what you propose," Steve mused. "McDonald's shall retain the currency it has unjustly captured, and we shall all underachieve perpetually in an unending cycle of torment and failure, just as the beaver builds the dam that is washed away by the floods brought on by the melting icecaps in someplace that has melting icecaps."

"But, Sir Bill, the greed of the wealthy can't supersede the need of the healthy, and no matter how I try to reason it, what I have just spoken has no redeeming value in any parlance or relevance other than the fact that I have said it in rhythm."

Steve, dressed like the King of Hearts in a deck of playing cards, turned his back to the young woman, who was wearing a sky-blue burlap sack tied at the waste with a rope. She was covered in mud.

Steve threw a regal gaze offstage. "Miss Alice," he boomed.

"Yes, Sir Bill," the frail actress answered.

Steve snapped his body around to face the young starlet. "Very well," he said. "Then together we shall find the average of the beginning and the end, to find a compromise that most accurately approximates the position in which we take to the masses. Like the choppy moat that is created by the gods to protect us—the very, very, *very* rich—we shall create a moat to be for certain that this pornography of which I hate does not cause our legacies to grow deplored or wanted."

"Oh, Mister Bill, you are oh so popular. You are oh so charismatic. You . . . you . . ."

Steve and the young thespian raced toward each other, meeting first lip to lip, and then breast to tummy, as they were washed in a simple blue spotlight from the backstage crew. Steve held his young costar firmly by her shoulders and guided her away from him. "If you are wrong, Miss Alice . . .," Steve said and paused dramatically. He looked upward above the heads of the audience that sat in the upper balcony: ". . . we may never work in this town again."

"And we shall bring notoriety to our humble burg," she said. She slowly turned her head to look out above the audience just as Steve had.

"Or infamy," Steve Martin said.

The blue spot vanished, and the curtain dropped on Miss Alice and Mr. Bill. The crowd sat with mouths agape. The power of the performances had stunned the audience. After a beat, they stood as one and showered the play and its actors with the adoration of wild applause, cheers and whistles.

Backstage, Navin—with a clipboard and a flashlight—

shook Steve's hand. "Brilliant, Steve," Navin said.

"Thank you," Steve said.

"And, Holly," Navin said to the redheaded actress, "that was spectacular."

"Thank you, Navin," Holly said. Her green eyes fixed onto his. After a moment, she looked to the floor as if she were embarrassed to realize that she stood before him naked.

"Hey, Holly," Navin said above the cheers from the theater, "how about that drink, maybe, uh, tonight?"

Holly's eyes rose and sparkled at Navin. "I think that would be nice," she said sheepishly.

"Really, Navin?" Steve interjected. "You're in the mood with all the weddings this weekend?"

"Weddings?" Navin asked.

"Jess, Suzy, Audrey," Steve said "The three-fer. You know . . .," Steve paused. "Ewwwwwww. You probably *don't* know."

"What?" Navin said.

"Yeah," Steve said. "They probably thought it best not to invite you. Suzy and Audrey are getting married, and Jess is renewing her vows with Russell in the same ceremony."

Navin looked to Holly.

"Oh, yeah," Holly said, perking up and suddenly feeling clothed. "I can't tonight. Drinks with you, I mean. I'm their maid of honor, and the Cindies are the bridesmaids. Didn't you used to date all of them, or something crazy and tormenting like that?"

"All the Cindies?" Navin asked, hoping to conceal a pang of pain.

"Ha!" Steve said. "No, Holly, he dated all the brides. That must suck eggs."

"They had to rent an entire Marriott hotel for tonight's dinner alone," Holly said. "I don't know how Geoff didn't tell you."

"Geoff knew?" Navin said.

Suddenly, the stage lights brightened and the crowd's roar shook the theater. Steve leaned into Navin's ear and yelled, "Gotta do the curtain call!" Steve took Holly's hand and pulled her in trot back onto the stage for one last round of bows and accolades.

The crowd's applause and whistles drifted from Navin's cognizance. Steve and Holly's bows dragged into slow motion, as Steve's royal gown and Holly's serf-ish garb waved majestically from the wind of a backstage fan. Navin peeked into the audience to see Geoff standing amongst three of the most recent Cindies, four rows from the stage. Geoff was wearing a tuxedo and wiping his nose. The Cindies wore navy-blue satin bridesmaid gowns. Their applause for Steve and Holly was enthusiastic and animated.

Navin spotted Jess and Russell embraced in a kiss two rows behind the Cindies and Geoff. "How can she come here knowing I am here," he thought.

Steve and Holly completed their bows, turned toward Navin, walked in his direction and smiled broadly. He felt a frown tug his mouth down toward his chin.

A small child rushed past Navin from behind, brushing the outside of his thigh as he raced by, to leap into Steve's arms. As Navin turned to see where he came from, he saw Audrey arm-in-arm with a handsome, well-fashioned man. The child, he assumed, was the stranger's. Without realizing it, Navin began to stride backward from the scene and out of the light.

The overload was oppressive: Jess, Audrey, Steve, Geoff, at least three of the Cindies, Russell, a child, a stranger, a girl named Holly who apparently knew him, an absurd play that followed a strange-but-vaguely-familiar verse, and an official clipboard that indicated Navin might be orchestrating his own demise.

When Navin awoke, he concluded he was the stooge.

There was no escape. He assumed it would be impossible to repay a debt he could not identify. In this dream, he knew he would be a prisoner to his failures until a chance at true redemption emerged. He feared that as long as his brain worked and he was alone, he would be imprisoned by his past.

※

"You're dreaming about Steve Martin?" Sid asked Navin over the phone.

"Yes," Navin said.

"And Winston Churchill?"

"Just once."

"And three women who are gone?" Sid asked.

"Yes."

"And their boyfriends?"

"Yes."

"And children not yet born, and women not yet met, and theaters with lame plays?"

"Yes."

"Starring Steve Martin?"

"Yes," Navin confirmed. Each held their phones to their ears as their eyes mindlessly scanned their surroundings. Navin's gaze hung anxiously as he awaited Sid's take—a take which Navin was certain would be terse, poignant and spot on. Instead, Sid posed a question.

"Who did you love most?" he asked. "Jess, Suzy or Audrey?"

"Wow," Navin said. "I have never thought of it that way."

"Well, think about it. I'll be there in a couple days."

☙

"And, so, who?" Geoff asked.

"It's not a matter of who I loved more, Geoff," Navin said.

"Well, it might not rewrite your tortured history, but it's a pretty good question," Geoff insisted.

"It doesn't matter, Geoff."

"It *does* matter!"

"Well, I told Sid I'd think about it."

"So, you'll think about it because he would like to know; or you'll think about it because you think it's relative; or you'll think about it because you want me to drop it—"

"The first one and the last one," Navin interrupted.

Geoff reached for a Buffalo wing from the paper-boat tray at the table's center. Navin looked up at the large projected image of a basketball game. "With all of this shit about how you can't keep a girl in your life, maybe you should look at things a little differently," Geoff said.

"OK," Navin snapped. His patience evaporated in the heat of his emotion. "Here's the deal: I was bored of Suzy, found comfort in Jess, and thought Audrey was a settlement I had to make."

"A settlement?" Geoff asked, licking the wing sauce from his fingers.

"Yes, a settlement. A last chance at a beautiful girl—a career girl, some status. And I settled for her not being nice to me, not being appreciative, not being thoughtful, not being grateful. I mean, I accepted all of that because it was better than nothing, and it was a known quantity—no surprises. And I had someone who could turn me on and made other guys jealous. A beautiful companion one or two nights a week." Navin looked to the table, back to the game on the wall, and then to Geoff.

"And what was Jess?"

"A fucking mistake. A sleepwalk. A recovery."

"And Suzy?"

Navin thought for a moment and gave a sigh. "I don't know," he said. "I wish I knew. Maybe she was home, once."

Geoff pulled another chicken wing from the paper boat and inserted the entire morsel long ways into his mouth. He clamped his upper and lower front teeth onto the wing just at his fingertips and pulled the wing outward, stripping it of all its meat.

"How do you not gain weight?" Navin asked, welcoming a chance to change the subject.

"I masturbate a lot," Geoff said as sauce seeped from between his lips. "A lot." He took a gulp of his beer. "That's all just retrospect. You've put them in categories based on hindsight, not how you were feeling at the time."

"So, your point?" Navin asked.

"My point is that as unhappy as you think you were with each of them now, you had made peace with being with them at the time. You made a deal."

"Bullshit," Navin said.

"Not bullshit," Geoff snapped. "Really, who the fuck do you think you are?"

"Don't start with this again—"

"I never stopped with it!" Geoff blurted. "Because you don't get it. There is something wrong with you.

There is a reason you are alone. There is a reason you always stress out and are a victim of your own thinking. You're an asshole to yourself."

Navin sighed. He knew that he was his worst critic.

"You are so obnoxious about what you want, Navin. But you play victim when you can't have it. You can't have it both ways."

"Why do you think you have this pinned down?" Navin asked.

"Because as I sit here and watch girl after girl come in and out of your life, all I am looking for is a single date. Just one Cindy to say yes. Maybe just one to come to my apartment to hang out. To come in when they pick up a ticket to a concert I got for them. To want to be there. Maybe to be there in the morning. And it sucks to talk about me, because there is nothing to talk about. That's why we're a match as friends: All you do is talk about yourself, and mope."

Navin stammered. His stomach flitted upside down and back again. He felt a true, deep pain. It occurred to him that he had spent most of his recent years holding up a mirror to himself because he thought that it would thwart uninvited criticism from his friends. He had employed his own version of Geoff's mentally killing off of his parents to control the inevitable blow. Sadly, he had just learned this strategy worked all too well. Frightened to hear an answer to what he was about to ask, Navin asked anyway: "Like, what have I said?"

Geoff paused and spoke carefully. "Audrey once broke up with a guy because he bought a shirt at Kohl's," he said. "It was beneath her to be seen with a guy who bought off the rack at a discount retailer. You tried to rub her head the morning after you first nailed her, and she told you she wasn't a dog, so stop. She was an ice queen."

"*Nailed* her?" Navin asked.

"You knew this early on, and still you spent months trying to make that work out; tried to be OK with her being mean to you. Living with it and bitching about it is the deal you made."

Navin gave a grin.

"What?" Geoff asked.

"Sounds silly now," Navin said. "But I—"

"You still embraced the good stuff," Geoff finished. "That's you. You fall on grenades."

Navin sighed. "And Jess?"

"What about her?" Geoff asked.

"What did you see there?"

"Well, nothing, because you tried to keep it a secret,

but we all knew. Fuck, Navin, Russell knew." Geoff immediately winced at his words, and his lips pursed as if he had tried to pull them back. Both froze.

"What?" Navin asked quietly as he looked over Geoff's shoulder to the wall.

Geoff paused and drew a breath. "He knew, Navin," he said. "Why do you think he changed jobs? Why do you think it was a no-brainer for Jess to leave you for him? Why do you think she just went away? You don't think they talked about this? Text-messaged alibis from foreign countries don't go unnoticed on cell phone bills. She was careless, and you were blind."

"Oh my god," Navin said. "She never . . . And others?"

"Phone bills, Navin. Russell started asking around. Then rumors. Then it was easy."

Navin looked to the table. "Everyone knew . . . Fuck me. And you. Phone bills?"

"No, that's not how I knew. And not because there was a glow when you were together. Or that you would leave parties at the same time, or that we saw her kissing you in the parking lot. Most of us knew because Jess was stupid. She is just a really stupid girl."

Navin cocked his head. Despite his shock, Geoff's account that Russell knew seemed familiar—as if he had once dreamt it. He gave a look that asked for an explanation. "Because of the text messages?" he asked.

"No, because when she said or did stupid shit, you always looked embarrassed. That was the giveaway. You did a masterful job of covering everything else. What you couldn't cover was . . ."

Geoff's voice began to fade and his lip began to quiver, and so he paused. Navin leaned in and stared intently at him to see what thought had been formed, but not yet been said.

"What you couldn't cover was the body language that accompanied your thought—'I am so glad people don't know we're having an affair. She's an idiot.' "

Navin and Geoff locked eyes. Neither felt uncomfortable in the gaze. Rather, somehow each recognized this was an important moment, and Navin feared more bombs were coming. "What?" he asked gently.

Geoff said nothing.

"What? Geoff, tell me."

"I wouldn't have been, Navin. I wouldn't have been embarrassed by her. It killed me to see you not tolerate this married woman who risked so much to be with you. I watched it the whole time. Your arrogance and your outward pride defied how good of a man you are. And there was Jess, attracted to that. He came back because he knew he was losing her, not because she was leaving him. But she would have left him for you. You never let her know. She loved you. I wished I was you then. And you were simply a prick. I saw you wasting it. You were happy by accident."

Navin drew a breath and held it for a moment. The basketball game on the wall had either ended or gone into halftime, as the television now showed a panel of bloated analysts speaking and gesturing from behind a desk. Either way, when Navin looked around, the room was slightly darker as evening had come. The clientele had turned over from a happy-hour crowd to an evening patronage, and the wait staff had changed shifts. Navin recognized all of this, but that discovery was quickly forgotten.

The news that Geoff wanted Jess overshadowed the shock that Russell had known about the affair. In a moment of self-preservation, Navin left the shock caused by his learning about Russell's knowledge and Jess' carelessness to simmer on the backburner. He sensed that everything contained in his skin had been scraped away. He had been turned inside out months ago. His cuts were exposed to the ocean salt, and his nudity had been on display without him ever knowing it. He had been parading around the gala with his zipper down and spinach in his teeth. He smiled and charmed, but only looked silly and pathetic. And as no one told him about his downed fly and blemished smile, nearly all of his friends had disappeared since Jess left him. He was abandoned. They had left him to grow lonesome and undignified. Invitations and phone calls stopped coming. And now he knew why.

As he left the pot that contained all this retrospective shame and regret to boil, he willed his concerns to focus upon his friend. "You loved Jess?" Navin asked.

"I did," Geoff said. "I really, truly did. And do. She's an idiot. She is no Cindy."

FATE | 10

NAVIN'S HEAD HUNG above the bathroom sink as mucus bungeed from his nose. His eyes were swollen shut from his tears. His breath was heavy and his chest heaved. The front tail of his t-shirt was saturated with tears from wiping his eyes and snot from blowing his nose. A sock hung loosely from his left foot. His pants were hung too low below his waist, which caused him to step on the bottoms of his pant legs when he paced the bathroom floor. His face was red from screaming, and his voice had become harsh and raspy.

His vision was starred from the pressure behind his eyes and distorted from his tears. He looked up to the mirror and through these eyes he saw a weathered face return a hateful gaze. His blue irises were encircled and abutted by pink rings and it made him look beaten.

"Fuck you!" he shouted. "You can't do this! You can't win at this! You can't be the guy you're not! You can't! You can't! You can't be likable when you think you're better than everyone else! You can't keep anyone in your life because they see through you . . ."

And so it went. With each new and careless insult and scream, he slipped further into sadness and frustration. Geoff had verified to him a side that he knew all too well: His terror was caused by acknowledging he had never really fooled anyone. That the price was higher than he ever knew. He knew he didn't have it together, and tonight he admitted that others knew he didn't. He had remained oblivious to the judgment he had hoped he escaped.

He paced his apartment asking aloud "why" and "why not." At times, his thoughts lead to tearful outbursts. At times, his thoughts calmed him. He was desperate to hide from himself, perhaps as he hid from strangers through a persona he knew to be false. The solitude in his apartment left him with company he did not particularly enjoy. To escape himself, he opened a small closet's door and tossed the shoes and the garments that had fallen to the floor from the hangers above into his bedroom. He crawled into the closet and lay on his side.

He cried and screamed until he could no longer, until his voice was nearly gone, until he had understood that he had senselessly ridiculed himself into embarrassment, until the dog on the first floor below began to bay. "Why," he asked aloud, "have I done this to myself?" He took a breath and, spent from the tantrum, tried to calm down. He was surrounded by darkness within the nearly shut closet. The only light pierced through the crack he had left by not closing the door completely. From the floor, he looked up to the mound of clothes and shoes that lay just beyond the door's opening. With his vision having cleared, he began to study the immediate changes in perspective one is afforded when one eye is closed. He closed his left eye, reopened it, and then closed his right eye. The objects beyond the crack jumped slightly in their positions.

He thought of all the times he spoke to Russell, not thinking that he knew. He could not imagine the hate Russell held but hid. He could not fathom that Russell never confronted him. But he didn't and, as it turned out, he didn't need to. The universe would. And it did. On this night.

Beyond the mound of clothes and shoes, the cast-iron bathtub beckoned. "Maybe I'll fill that thing up and see what happens," he said. Then he smiled, having made himself laugh.

☙

Steve Martin awoke, lying naked on his back beneath the covers of a near-stranger's bed in a near-stranger's bedroom. Over his thighs, atop the covers, was the naked right leg of a beautiful thirty-something woman. Her nude breasts were pressed against his right side. Her head rested on his chest. His right hand held her right shoulder, and her right arm crossed his body to hold his left elbow.

Behind her, on the opposite side of the bed, was a three-year-old boy who rested his chin in the palm of his hand. The boy seemed unfazed by the scene and peered over his sleeping mother's soft, china-white shoulders directly into Steve Martin's eyes.

Steve took a slow, heavy gulp. Though he knew that he had known this woman for a few weeks, and knew that intimacy would likely happen after their date the night before, he suddenly felt the woman he had been courting was a complete stranger. He had not known that a child might live in this house. Or that she might even have a child. Or that this child might climb into bed with him just moments after he had considered waking his mother because of his self-governing morning erection. None of these things, Steve thought, could have been predicted.

Steve pulled the covers as close to his chin as he could. The sleeping beauty's weight pinned the blankets to his body, but still Steve was able to gain a couple extra inches of cover. Steve occasionally peeked to the boy to see what he was doing. The boy looked bored, but patient and content. His gaze never left Steve. The woman, on the other hand, was very much asleep.

Steve closed his eyes in hopes that the boy might think that he too was sleeping, and perhaps get bored and go to another room. Certainly the last thing Steve Martin wanted—in this situation—was a conversation with a three-year-old boy. He hoped to awaken her, so he closed his eyes and began to tighten his embrace around her neck, all while not letting the boy catch on that he was awake and available for idle chitchat.

The child's curiosity pulled him around the foot of the bed to stand next to Steve. He took a position and stared at Steve until it became, seemingly, lunchtime. Steve felt the child's gaze, and at times could smell his breath. As much as he tried to not open his eyes, he did, and he released an admitting sigh.

"Why is Mommy holding your elbow?" the boy asked, breaking the morning silence and sending a jolt through Steve Martin's abdomen.

"Ummm," Steve said quietly, "so it doesn't fall off."

"Oh," the unmoved three-year-old said. The boy looked around and drew a deep, confused breath. "Why is Mommy's leg there like that?"

"Ummm," Steve whispered, deathly afraid of what the next question might be. "So it doesn't fall off," he said slowly.

Satisfied with those answers and seemingly uninterested in anything else with regard to body positions or nudity, the boy looked around the room before returning his gaze to Steve. "What's your name?" the boy asked.

"I'm Martin," Steve said. "Martin Short."

"Is that your gum, Martin?" the boy asked.

"What gum?"

"Over there," the boy said while pointing at a square pack of gum that was neatly stacked atop a square tin box of cinnamon Altoids on the dresser.

"Yes, it is," Steve said.

"Can I have a piece?" the boy asked.

Steve thought for a moment. "You'll have to ask your mother."

"But she's sleeping."

"Maybe you could wake her up and ask," Steve suggested strategically.

The boy looked at the woman, and back at Steve. "I don't want to, Martin."

Steve pulled and tugged at the covers to bring them closer to his chin. He heard paper rustle and looked to see that the boy had already broken a square piece of gum through the bubble foil and began chewing. Steve sunk further beneath the covers as the boy's chewing grew louder, wetter and smackier. Imprisoned naked beneath the woman's dead-weighted cuddle, Steve quickly grew annoyed with the boy's open-mouthed chewing and felt helpless in his ability to find an escape without the aid of the comatose mother.

"Hey," Steve said in an excited tone that suggested he had just had a pleasant epiphany that would yield the boy an exciting start to his day. "Why don't you go to the bathroom and brush your teeth, then go to your room and pick out some clothes to wear today? That way . . . we can . . . or I can . . . get a taxi . . . and maybe you can tell . . . Mommy. . . that Martin . . . got in it . . . and . . ."

"I don't want to," the boy said, smacking his lips.

"Oh," Steve said looking down toward his feet, which were spaced about two feet apart with the toes pointed toward the ceiling. Steve raised his gaze to the ceiling fan, and at the ochre-colored, water-damage veins that had bled through the paint of this older Hollywood Hills house. He looked down to the sleeping woman's head. She was breathing harder now and was in a much deeper sleep. He turned to see that the boy was still chewing his gum and was staring at him. They looked at each other for a time—the boy without expression, and Steve with uncertain fear.

"Does your elbow fall off a lot, Martin?" the boy asked.

"No," Steve said, looking back toward the ceiling. "Not as much as it used to."

"Did it hurt when it used to fall off, Martin?"

"No, not really," Steve said.

"Do other parts of you fall off, Martin?"

"No, not until today."

"Mommy says if I unscrew my belly button, my butt will fall off. Does your butt fall off, Martin?"

"It probably did this morning."

"Can I see, Martin?"

"No."

"OK."

The woman twisted a bit and released a relaxed hum. She slid her right knee down his leg and removed her hand from Steve's left elbow. Steve, sensing an opportunity to gain her assistance in having the boy leave for just enough time for him to put on clothes, said softly, "Good morning." The woman, not really ever awake, placed her right hand on Steve's groin, softly humped his side twice, and began to snore.

"Do want some gum, Martin?" the boy asked.

"No, uh, no," Steve said.

The boy pursed his lips and looked at his sleeping mom. He looked at the television that sat atop the dresser and then across Steve's chest to the closet. He stared aimlessly at the closet, lifted his right hand to his face and stuck his index finger up his nose. He removed his finger and looked at his fingertip, finding nothing, then looked back at Steve and sighed. "How about a mint?" he asked.

"Those are some fucked-up dreams," Geoff said as he and Navin sat in beach chairs on the Palm Beach sand. "What does your therapist say?"

"He's entertained," Navin said, "I think."

"But you're having sex dreams about Steve Martin."

"No," Navin quickly said. "I had a dream about him in a difficult situation. There was no sex in that dream."

"Yeah, you're right."

Geoff pointed his nose to the high sun and closed his eyes. "So, let's recap."

"No, let's not," Navin said. "We recapped yesterday, and now I'm more depressed."

"No, not about your shit," Geoff said. "About this whole Steve Martin's journal thing."

"That's *becoming* my shit," Navin said. "It is my shit."

"Exactly! You found this journal, it's got your imagination running wild, your life sucks because you're about to get a fauxhawk and a sports car. It's all connected. You're processing!"

"Mmm, maybe."

"So—"

"No, stop. Enough stomping for land mines. I don't like what I'm finding."

"No, listen . . .," Geoff insisted. "You had a daydream

that Steve Martin funnied Audrey to death in a New York restaurant; a dream that he was nailing your mom—"

"Nailing?"

"Sorry," Geoff said quickly, ". . . and was going to kill you and Lee Harvey Oswald. And, now, a dream that he is in bed with a chick he's nailed—"

"Nailed? What is it with you and the word 'nailed?' "

"I like that word," Geoff said, ". . . and some weird gum-chewing, booger-picking, staring kid gawks at Steve and offers him one of his own Altoids."

"Don't even start going into a childhood analysis," Navin said.

"No, that's for David to do."

"Yes, that's why I pay David."

"I'm just saying—and this is coming from the hopeless, tall, skinny guy that idolizes the normal, tortured guy—that this is something big for you."

"You're making too much of this."

"Maybe you're not making enough of it." The two looked toward the sea and saw a mother and her little boy building a sandcastle. "Listen, what were you thinking about just before you went to sleep last night?"

"Suicide."

"What?!"

"Not seriously—relax. Death by bathing. I suspect that if I take a bath in that cast-iron tub, the floor won't hold the weight and I'll crash to the unit below and die naked and wet, taking that dog with me. It's a funny thought."

"It's not a funny thought. What led to that?"

"Stop it!" Navin demanded. "Stop asking questions!"

Geoff retreated for a moment. "Well, if you die this week, I'll tell Steve Martin you found his journal."

"Will you?" Navin paused for a moment and said, "I'm sure he will be relieved that it is safely in the hands of a very stable, very content, very sane person." He turned and stretched in his chair. "This is all I'll tell you: I got very, very sad last night. Very emotional. And it was all about what we talked about yesterday. It's a tough reality to face."

"And so you dreamt about Steve Martin naked in bed with a three-year-old boy."

"No, that wasn't what the dream was about," Navin said defensively.

"I'm sure the authorities might see that differently," Geoff said laughing. "OK, so—"

"Knock it off already! There is no link. I can't find one. I've looked," Navin said with a grin. "But there is one Steve Martin thing in the back of my mind. It might be why he keeps popping up when it makes no sense."

"What?"

"A verse—a verse that is in Steve Martin's journal."

"Satanic?"

"It's Steve Martin, you tool, not Salman Rushdie. Do you really envision a fatwa being issued against 'The Lonely Guy'?"

"Well, there was 'Novocaine.' "

"Good point."

"A verse?"

"Yes, a verse. I think it's fascinating. It's like being privileged enough to be let in on the genesis of a piece of art—like knowing what the premise is, the process, where it goes. Like being in the room when van Gogh painted the first marks on a canvas, or when Mozart placed the first note on a scale. The entire journal seems so innocuous, except for this one verse."

"What's it say?"

"I don't know. I mean, I don't know what it means. It sounds Shakespearian to me or something."

"Do you have it?"

"Eh! Star like charmer hated porno. If wrong be, I am wanted and deplored. The warm town inhabits, earns TV time."

"You memorized it?"

"Yeah, and I didn't tell you but I had a dream about this, too. Steve Martin was acting in a silly stage play that resembled the verse."

"Shakespeare, porno and TV time?"

"Sounds crazy, yes?"

"Yes. And the dream?"

"I don't want to tell you."

"Why not?"

"You'll try to connect dots that don't connect."

"Audrey was in the dream?"

"Yes."

"Jess?"

"Yes."

"Suzy, too?"

"Yes."

"Shit!" Geoff said.

"And you, and a few of the Cindies," Navin offered.

"What?"

"And all of their new husbands and boyfriends and, in some cases, children."

"All of them *and* Steve Martin?"

"Yes."

"Fuck!" Geoff thought for a moment. "And your mom?

Was Steve Martin nailing your mom in the dream?"

"Geoff! Um, well," he said as he realized the relevance of Geoff's question. "Now that you mention it, I don't recall Mom being in the dream at all."

"Well, there you go, then."

"What?"

"Your mom is the curse of all your relationships, and Steve Martin's verse has made you realize it."

"Get lost!"

"Navin! You faced everything in that dream except your mom."

"I don't lose sleep over my mom," Navin snapped. "I lose sleep over everything else."

"Your mind is protecting you, Navin. And God placed Steve Martin's journal on a pile of plowed snow in New York so we can sit here on the beach at this very moment and figure you out."

"God?" Navin challenged.

"OK, *Cliff*, if you prefer."

Navin sat on his sofa in the early evening with the satisfaction of absorbing just the right amount of sun.

The weather was perfect for South Florida. A breeze moved the curtains that guarded the open living room window. The off-tempo beats of the drapes flapping like a flag relaxed him, and the breeze stroked him and gave him attention.

Reaching for his laptop, he anxiously checked his email for Sid's itinerary. He also hoped to discover some interest from his online dating subscriptions.

He logged into his email account, cautiously skimmed through and deleted the junk mail that promised harder erections, longer staying power and bargain-basement prices on fake Rolex watches. He was cautious when he deleted this spam because he deemed it necessary. He reviewed the body of each email in the event his eternal soul mate and match might be named Ginger Steele or Pen S. Strong. He must prevent carelessness from causing him to throw eternal happiness into a trashcan icon on his laptop.

"NAVIN," the booming voice of God bellowed as Navin, dressed in a linen robe and sandals, stood before the Almighty. "You've questioned me your entire life. You've doubted and cursed me. Your faith has been weak. You have spread your faithlessness

to others through drunken diatribes—usually at funerals, or while watching television commercials that feature Sally Struthers, or movies that starred Corey Feldman. And, worse yet, you carelessly tossed aside the one who would provide the bliss that is my kingdom—love, family, peace within your heart. You deleted her, Navin—Candy Stripper. Because you thought that it was a solicitation—an advertisement for the remedy for a tiny penis. As so many others, Navin, you missed life because you thought your cock was large enough. The esteem in which you held your cock, Navin, has not served you well. And, therefore, you missed my greatest gift of all. Sure, it was unfortunate that her name was Candy Stripper. But, hey, we all have our things. Candy was your salvation, Navin. Your lifelong crisis in faith in her—and, therefore, me—shall place you into damnation. Eternally. I'm sorry, my lost sheep."

So Navin was sure to open each email before he trashed it. This gave spammers across the universe a market for their wares, even if such a market was viewing out of the fear of eternal regret.

Thirty-three new emails filled his inbox. Thirty-two offered penile improvements, while one offered a website link to new and exciting sexual positions. There were no emails from interested online daters, however, nor an update from Sid about his travel plans.

He began his search for online news. He sat on his sofa and propped his feet up onto a coffee table littered with unopened mail, and DVDs and empty cases that he had someday hoped to reunite and store in boxes. The sea breeze from the window rhythmically blew across his body some more as he punched the laptop's keys. The sleeves of his t-shirt flapped in the wind and brushed against him, caressing him and causing an occasional outbreak of goose bumps. He relished how the breeze soothed his body, like water.

There was no political or world news unique from the norm. In entertainment, however, Navin paused on the story that Pope St. Frances of Assisi John Mark Judas IV had attended the funeral of an Italian crooner who had recently passed. Also in attendance were several heads of state, global celebrity giants from the entertainment industry, and Antony Brunopulcelli-Cabonolli. Brunopulcelli-Cabonolli was the first sub-five-foot-six-inch, first-generation National Basketball Association player of Italian descent who had won the professional league's Most Valuable Player award in back-to-back seasons. Though Navin was not much of a sports fan, he did recall seeing highlights of this tiny basketball player's uniform with the name A. Brunopulcelli-Cabonolli arced above his trademarked uniform number 88. The "A," Navin later learned, was required by the league because there was a Carmine Brunopulcelli-Cabonolli who also played in the league, though in a different conference. Carmine Brunopulcelli-Cabonolli wore number 1; was seven-feet-two-and-a-half inches tall; played for a team that, wisely, did not put their players' names on their uniforms; and was of no relation to Antony.

The story later noted that this crooner's credits included a melodic rendition of Madonna's "Lucky Star" that climbed the music charts around much of the globe. The recording was completely obscure in the United States, and had only briefly cracked the top twenty-five in most of the Middle East. But, it did hold the number-one spot in Japan for a record fifty-nine consecutive weeks.

In the ongoing "Bonzo" custody case, Latin pop sensation Gonzo Chavez failed to attend a custody hearing after learning that Bonnie Jasper was a person of interest in the disappearance of Francis—the one-armed, fifty-two-year-old subject of the custody battle between the two. A left leg, as determined by the fact that the big toe of the foot was located farthest right when it was held upright, had been found on Francis' estate. The leg was being tested to determine whose leg it was. Early media speculation was that it had most recently been attached to the already uni-armed Francis.

Navin's amusement abruptly turned to shock and introspection upon reading that the older Hungarian man—who had awoken from an eighteen-year coma—and his wife had died instantly when the ambulance that was taking them home was t-boned in an intersection just moments after leaving the Budapest hospital. They had lived in the facility for nearly two decades—he in a coma, and she duteously near his side. Navin felt a pit in his stomach. The comfort from the breeze vanished and the computer on his lap grew hot, uncomfortable and invasive.

"There can't be a God," he. "It's just not possible."

He raised his eyes and stared straight ahead at nothing. Then he stood with no specific plan to go someplace else in his apartment, because anywhere else would do.

☙

Navin returned from the kitchen with a bottle of water and a bowl of corn chips. Freshly showered and dressed in a loosely fitting linen shirt and a pair of linen pajama pants, he returned to his sofa and laptop and the disorganized layer of outdated media that sprawled on his coffee table. He slapped the space bar to awaken his computer, made some room on the table for his water and reclined on the sofa to go online.

As his computer awoke, he realized he had little recollection of the shower he had just taken. A shower was a simple step, it seemed, in getting through any day; in biding the time that had to pass before something more meaningful could impact his life. It was an exercise of maintenance, he thought, akin to brushing his teeth or eating breakfast. These things required time and diligence to maintain who he was, but not improve it. A lot of time, he reasoned, was spent to avoid getting worse.

He appreciated this last shower as something needful. As his computer screen began to flicker to life, he thought how this shower afforded the pause to heal. He had basked in the sensation of the water falling over his head, creeping onto his shoulders and flowing down his back. He stood motionless as the warmth washed away his tears and the splashes drowned his sobs. The sensations relaxed his mind. His thoughts flew freely without agenda. The water coated and held him. He had returned to the womb.

The news of the Hungarian husband and wife shocked him. The news reported a cruel and unjust event. But it caused him to seek a new perspective: to find a way to accept how the world, a tough place indeed, worked.

He did not believe in an afterlife, but was fearful of one. Sid influenced his belief on this question. In Sid's view, "We die and turn to dirt, and that's it." Just as the simple thought of an afterlife comforted many who sought an explanation to the unknown, Sid had given Navin an equally as uninvolved answer to mankind's greatest mystery. But Navin remained a romantic, and for all of his cynicism he was, at heart, an optimist for all things.

He had reasoned that the auto accident in Hungary was an act of compassion by a higher power—a higher power in whom or what he had not ever believed, but truly wanted. The crash was for the sake of art amongst the living. This tragedy was meant for all who care to ponder such things. For the couple whose love had fueled an improbable reunion, their reward came with the fate of death—instantly, unforeseen and together. What happens after that, he rationalized, is not in our grasp, nor is it ours to know. But perhaps the story wasn't as tragic as it appeared at first blush: Maybe in this death there was reward. Perhaps that was their role in this universe. Maybe their legacy would be the touching of others as they had touched Navin. It could be that in dust we become nothing at all. Nothing. And in this couple's reduction to nothing, their last feeling, final reality, true realization of a magnificent destiny was the joy they shared in their final moments. No pain. No worry. Their demise was only known to the living. Their deaths were never really known to them. They only knew redemption and reward. They only knew their happily ever after.

Navin turned off the shower and surrounded himself with a clean, white robe.

"A perfect end," he thought.

IMPORTED BEER | 11

NAVIN'S COMPUTER GREETED him with three new emails, none of which contained vulgar solicitations. Two were from vendors; one a commercial script writer; and the other a graphic artist. The third was from Sid. Sid was arriving the next day. Navin grew excited. "Yes, I can pick you up at the airport," Navin replied. "I'm not working for a couple weeks . . . or longer. See you then."

There were also no responses to his latest online dating profile. It seemed that simply stating "I'm a good guy" wasn't creating any buzz. For a moment, he considered rewriting his profile yet again, but decided it wasn't worth his time.

An online crossword puzzle beckoned, but his failure to answer any of the first eight clues discouraged him and so he stopped. He was also reluctant to read the news. He had already processed what he had learned that day to an acceptable conclusion and was reluctant to undo it. Navin was bored, and that lead to an unhealthy drift toward exploring his hard drive.

His computer contained thousands of photographs from his life. Many pictures were of either him and Jess, or him and Audrey. They were all from his happiest days. He shared his love for escape with each and documented their happiness—more than most would—through photography. These were memories, however, that he could not view. These were images of a person he could barely remember himself being. The images of Audrey and Jess were reminders of women in love with him, and that image seemed impossible now.

He had avoided viewing the photos of him and Jess. As a child who learns about the heat from a stovetop burner, he knew that going to that place would scald.

But with Audrey, he thought he could reclaim these memories as his own. She was an invited guest into his world. He had authored that happiness. Plus, Audrey's rap sheet was incriminating to her character. The petulance she displayed toward him over their final weeks gave him the courage to open the desktop folders that contained the only proof of that better time. It was a time he missed, and to which he wanted to return. After a beat, he took a deep breath and opened the folder.

The photos were stunning: perfectly sunlit landscapes, monuments, and slices of life on the streets of the globe's greatest cities. The memories of those days commanded his attention in the most melancholy of ways. Every so often he would reach a photo of him and Audrey, or just she alone, and the melancholy turned to bittersweet sadness, and then longing. The happiness that shone through on each of their faces, or in their body language, in each photo was pure. "How can that just go away?" he asked.

He had discovered images of himself happy, and studied his own eyes. She glowed. The photos of the two of them together could not have been matched by any other couple in any other era—not Romeo and Juliet, nor Abelard and Heloise. Knowing her as he did now didn't matter. The atrocious qualities that he discovered defined her were nowhere in these photos. She was a beautiful, loving and bashful woman. The camera had filtered out everything about her that was anything less than perfect.

Navin had told Geoff just a day before that she

represented a sellout of sorts to him. These photos called him out on the rationalization that enabled him to remain his harshest critic. These snapshots that he carried with him everywhere, but never viewed, captured his dream. He realized this relationship was never a sellout at all. It was as it should have been.

In these shots he was, indeed, living for another. He was gifting happiness. He was sharing his joy. Each looked as if they were falling in love along the Seine or atop the Cliffs of Moher. But the storybook that these photos should have illustrated was never written. The return trips to those places to rekindle that most coveted of feelings would never happen. And for that, he was sad. "It's a waste," he said.

Navin recalled that Bruce Springsteen once asked if dreams still live if they never come true. Navin hung onto this idea despite having proof of his dream being very much alive, if even for only a moment.

His wish had been granted in a specific place and a specific time, if only for a limited and specific duration. For someone who desired permanence it was a cruel, teasing taste. He recognized many of the images as those that randomly flickered through his consciousness during his panic attack nights before. His happiness was obligatorily linked to these memories of travel, and that travel was handcuffed to those with whom he had taken with him. Therefore, these memories of happier times were married to the heartbreak of later losing those relationships. These photos showed him he could live. They were relics. There were no living witnesses—no one left with whom to reminisce. No one remained who cherished these times as he had. He thought again of the question Springsteen had asked, and then asked his own: If the dream comes true but you are all that remains, then did it ever exist at all?

"I think I have it!" Geoff exclaimed on the phone.

"Have what?" Navin asked.

"The meaning of the verse—the verse from Steve Martin's journal."

"I never said there was a meaning," Navin said. "I only said it's cool to see the process, and that I wondered where it goes from here."

"Of course there's a meaning," Geoff said. "You found a journal, you found this verse. It means something."

Navin thought for a second and realized that it had been a few conversations since Geoff had bellyached about any one of the Cindies or the great McDonald's drive-thru conspiracy. He thought it best to roll with it. It was, after all, getting late. "OK, what?" he asked.

"It's so simple! You are meant to be with Audrey!" Geoff said.

"I am *not* meant to be with Audrey. She's the kind that might tell Winston Churchill to 'fuck off.'"

"Yes, you are. You told her you wouldn't call and you haven't. But now you can."

"Where do you get this?"

"Easy. You are the charmer, and she is the one that is wanted and deplored all at the same time. The warm town is here, where we live, and the TV time is all about Audrey's narcissism."

"That not only fails to make any sense, but it's a stretch, Geoff. I can apply that logic to anything."

"No, you can't."

"Yes, I can. I can make it fit your life, if you want."

"No, you can't because I didn't find the journal."

"No, I'm making a point that the verse is wide open. It's elusive; you can make it mean almost anything. I know! I've tried to figure it out! And, besides, your little translation of the thing is really, *really* not good."

"How?"

"What?"

"Not good how?"

"Well, you left out the porno thing."

"You had great sex with her, right?"

"That's not porno, that's—"

"You don't have to believe—"

"Look, it is simple. Steve Martin lost his journal and I found it."

"You said it yourself, that you think it came to you for a reason."

"I did."

Navin was growing annoyed at Geoff's flimsy knack for tailoring people's comments to feed his delusions and needs. And, in this seemingly meaningless twist on a simple verse, he felt the manipulation begin.

It took several years for Navin to begin to recognize Geoff's ability to reframe reality for his own benefit. Until recently, Geoff's banal games had been overlooked in favor of a life-long friendship.

Navin's efforts to pull Geoff along in life began early, when they met in middle school in their native St. Louis. Both were fairly unpopular, but Navin was a misunderstood independent: He was discovering The Police and the Talking Heads while others his age were just coming down from the "Grease" soundtrack and disco's waning punches.

Geoff, on the other hand, was just simply unlikeable.

Often, Navin's efforts saw him expend his personal capital. Most ploys and efforts backfired, causing him the embarrassment that Geoff truly deserved.

Geoff once told Navin about his plan to shoplift condoms on a weekend when Geoff thought he might lose his virginity. He was, like most were, too embarrassed to buy them. He explained he would cup the box in the palm of his hand and slide it into his front pocket. He would buy a few packs of gum and other assorted toiletries in order to actually pay for something to ease his guilt. Navin volunteered to buy them for him and, when he did, was caught by his grandmother. Grandma Peaches, a devout Catholic, asked all in her prayer group to pray for him. They did. And they judged, as well, and freely spoke of Grandma Peaches' teenage grandson in Sunday evening tithe-counting sessions.

Growing up, Geoff was fiercely afraid of his father. Navin had suspected that Geoff had been neglected by him, but Geoff never shared any stories. When Geoff was seventeen, he ran a stop sign and t-boned a passing car. Although the car he hit spun a quarter turn and slid about 15 yards, the driver, fearing something, drove off. With no witnesses, Navin took Geoff's place behind the wheel for when the police showed. In the shuffle, neither noticed that Geoff's baggie of marijuana had flown from the sprung glove compartment, and so Navin, yet again, took the blame and an eventual hike in his automobile-insurance policy rates, and an immediate reaction from his mother.

Navin moved to South Florida. Geoff showed up shortly thereafter. Geoff wouldn't leave Navin's apartment until Navin presented to him a bank teller job wrapped in an ultimatum. "You can't and won't be here all the time," Navin told him. But Geoff never really went anywhere.

Navin took in stride all of the predicaments that Geoff somehow roped him into. And so a bond, or obligation, strengthened.

There were also fun times: In their 20s, they often drank until they nearly couldn't walk and, upon stumbling upon a parking garage, would footrace to the top floor and piss over the ledge. The first to evacuate his bladder, Navin would proclaim, would be declared the winner.

Public fountains on drunken nights often hosted impromptu early morning swims. Late-night vandalism to public buildings, often in the form of smeared food items such as mashed potatoes, resulted in edible graffiti on hallway walls.

When Geoff's father died after a long bout with leukemia, Navin offered the only hand Geoff could hold. There was an unspoken pain to which Navin bore witness. There was a story that would never be told. And that untold and inexplicable tale was too strong a bond to be broken by common sense. Geoff had no one. And Navin took Geoff as his own and never counted the cost.

But Navin's memories that were once innocuous had started to retain a negative value, and they were summing to bitter resentment.

꿍

The phone rang and Navin answered. "Hello?"
"Hi, Navin. This is Steve Martin."
"Uh, hi, Steve."
"Did I wake you?"

"It's a little late, um, I was nodding off I guess . . ."

"Sorry. Well, listen, I just wanted to give you a call and tell you that you are a good man. Give yourself a break every once in a while, OK? Good night."

◊

"I dreamt Steve Martin called me last night," Navin said as he sat at the coffee counter, to Geoff's left.

"Yeah?" Geoff asked. "What'd he say?"

"He said I was a good man."

"And?"

"That was it."

Geoff sipped his coffee, and then Navin did as well. "Well," Geoff asked. "Do you believe him?"

◊

Airplanes formed a line toward the west as they approached Palm Beach International Airport. Navin drove beneath a jet about to land as he headed south on Military Trail while Sid sat in the passenger seat.

Sid's square jaw was framed by an equally square baseball cap with the embroidery of some unknown nautical flag. His goatee was silver and crisply trimmed. He wore khaki shorts, sandals and an untucked, solid-blue linen Tommy Bahama shirt. His round, wire-rimmed eyeglasses made him appear scholarly. The silver in his hair that flowed from beneath his cap told of his wisdom. His voice was clear and articulate. He often over-enunciated when he spoke, as if he were narrating an Animal Planet documentary.

Sid's son, Lindsey, was Navin's classmate at MICDS. Sid quickly grew fond of Navin, and saw something refreshingly cynical and joyfully frank about the boy. Sid built industrial parks in St. Louis until it no longer made sense to. So, then he built them in Chicago, Indianapolis, Louisville and Cincinnati. He built further east into the Rust Belt—Columbus, Toledo and Detroit. He doubled back and developed Wichita and Omaha. By the late 1980s, Sid's industrial park empire spanned enough of the continent to be known as Arrow National. But by the mid-1990s, communities—many of which featured unviable and hollowed out Main Street storefronts along lines of archaic parking meters—had grown suspect of out-of-town developers. The Wal-Mart phenomenon had shut down countless family-owned shoe stores and luggage shops. Dick, whose name appeared above a Main Street haberdashery, simply went away while his assistant of over 25 years could be found greeting customers while standing next to a parked train of royal-blue shopping carts.

Sid and his Arrow National brand had seemingly come to the end of their runs until, in the summer of 1998, Navin asked Sid how business was. Sid told him and, without as much as a pause, Navin calmly said, "Simple. Change your name to 'ARROW-YOUR-TOWN-HERE' and include an opulent public green in every development with a band shell, lake, Little League Baseball fields—everything tax payers want, but don't want to be taxed for."

And it was simply this simple. By 2004, and after a little polishing of the branding, Tulsa Arrow, Austin Arrow, Denver Arrow and dozens more had grown from orphaned land, providing tennis courts, skateboard parks and lighted jogging trails. And with that, Navin's thought had made Sid millions upon millions, stacked atop millions of dollars.

"I thought we'd hit this little hole in the wall down here," Navin said, ". . . if you're hungry."

"I am," Sid said.

"Hope you don't mind."

"Not at all."

"It's a real locals' place, but getting off the island is refreshing now and then," Navin said. They drove a bit further. "Actually, it's a shithole."

"I'm sure it's fine," Sid said. "It's clean, though, right?"

"I don't really know," Navin said. "It's pretty dark and dank in there."

Navin parked the car on the street in front of the restaurant. Sid noticed the road was lined with one- and two-story square buildings. Most of the doors were fronted by security bars. Grass and weeds crawled up from the breaks in the sidewalk's pavement. Litter blew across the street, and the cars that traveled this bit of road were often dented or had quarter panels or doors of a color that didn't match the rest of the vehicle. The road was flat and stretched in either direction without any variety at all.

The restaurant's deep-brown façade provided the only break from the street's monotony. A life-sized wooden seaman in a wooden yellow slicker, smoking a wooden tobacco pipe, gripping a wooden steering wheel stood sentry to the right side of the entrance. Neon signs advertising beer flickered in the windows, but were dulled by the deep tint of the glass. The windows were guarded with wrought-iron bars. Navin opened the door, inviting Sid in before him, and said, "Best not order the oysters."

The darkness inside pushed the bright Florida sun from their eyes and caused an extended period of blindness. The neon lights that hung in the window, however, were far brighter on the inside.

To the right, a bar lined the wall. To the left were a run of booths. "Booth fine?" Navin asked.

"Of course," Sid said.

"Can I get you something?" the woman behind the bar asked.

"Sid?" Navin offered.

"A Heineken, please," Sid requested.

"There's Budweiser, Miller Lite and Corona," the woman said.

"I'll have the import, then," Sid said.

"Me, too," Navin said.

The two men slid into benches on each side of the table and settled in for a look at each other.

"So, how are things?" Sid asked.

"OK," Navin said. "Tough few weeks, Sid. Just all catching up."

"What is?"

"I don't know, all of it I guess."

"Your whole life, or Audrey, or more?"

"More, I think," Navin said. "I don't know. But as much as I need to talk to you about this, I don't want to consume you."

"I knew what I was getting into, Navin. It's why I'm here."

"How?" Navin asked, flattered. "I mean, what made you think—"

"I hear it in your voice on the phone. I hear it in your voice when you write," Sid said.

Navin grinned at Sid's way of saying things. "In my voice when I write," he repeated.

"Yes."

"Here you go, boys," the woman said as she delivered the beers.

"Can I start a tab?" Sid asked.

"Probably," the woman said. "I don't work here."

"Fair enough," Sid said amused. His eyes followed the woman's path as she gathered her purse and car keys and left the bar. He looked to the menu, then looked to Navin. "You don't mind if I don't eat, do you?"

Navin laughed. "I prefer that you didn't."

"You know what I mean," Sid said, getting back to the matter at hand.

"I do," Navin said. "I know what you mean. I'm beginning to hear it when I breathe."

Sid took a drink of his beer. "So, which one?"

"I don't know, Sid," Navin said. "I thought about it a lot. My friend, Geoff, has tried to draw it out of me, too. I can't answer it."

"No answer, huh?"

"Not really." Navin drank as Sid's gaze never broke. "I tell you, though; I went through some photos last night. And I don't think I have ever been more in love with an idea than I was when I met Audrey."

"I read that email, Navin. *All* of it."

"You're a patient man," Navin said with a smile and saluted him by tipping the neck of his beer bottle toward him.

"That was really good," Sid said. "*Really* good. You said it all. You answered your own questions. You were assertive for yourself. You stood up for yourself. And you shared it with someone."

"That's what I was doing?" Navin asked. "I just thought I was bitching."

Sid took a drink. "It's OK to say you got fucked

every once in a while," he said. "It's not always your fault. In fact, it's usually nobody's fault."

"Yeah," Navin said, looking to the table.

"So, you couldn't pick one?" Sid asked.

"No, I couldn't."

"And I'll tell you why," Sid said. "Because you loved them all. It's not in your nature not to."

"But that doesn't mean anything, does it?"

"It does," Sid said. "It means you love, you've loved more than once, and that you will again."

"Yeah, but—" Navin said.

"Stop trying to turn the good times of your life into bad times," Sid said. "There's only one mistake you keep making." Sid's flair for the dramatic often involved making someone ask for his opinion.

"What is that, Sid?"

"You try out for their team as opposed to making them try out for yours," Sid said with an arrogant grin.

Navin took a drink.

"Do you still have that journal by Steve Martin?" Sid asked.

"I do."

"Have you had any dreams lately?"

"Last night."

"And?"

"I dreamt he called to tell me I am a good man."

"Anything else?"

"And that I should I give myself a break every once in a while."

Sid smiled and took another sip, swallowed hard and set the bottle on the table. "I think you should listen to him."

DEATH & LIFE | 12

"**HOW IS SID?**" Geoff asked.

"He's good," Navin said, out of breath from climbing the staircase to his apartment door.

"Did he ask about me?" Geoff asked.

"He doesn't know you," Navin said. He moved his phone from one ear to the other to allow his right hand to reach his pocket for his keys.

"Exactly," Geoff said.

"I get it," Navin said. "Maybe next time?"

"I'll hold my breath."

"Listen, I've got to run, I'll call you later."

"OK," Geoff said. "And when you guys fuck, will you think of me?"

"Goodbye, Geoff," Navin said, and ended the call. He reached the door, tugged the key from his front pants pocket and let himself into his apartment. Sid had to catch up with a lady friend for dinner at a French brasserie within The Breakers hotel and was going to come over to Navin's after.

The Breakers was an opulent property that, despite Navin's ability to mix in nearly any setting, made him uncomfortable. Its presumption was reinforced by its staff and verified by its clientele. He traced his unease to the fact that he was an admitted faux resident of Palm Beach, having secured a near-oceanfront apartment on the island for just twenty-four-hundred dollars per month—something less than guilt, but something more than pride.

Navin found an empty box in his closet and raked the coffee table clean of assorted papers, movies and trash. He did the same with every table and countertop, and placed the box on the closet floor on which he had broken down just a couple nights before.

A quick hand wash of the dishes and a cursory scrubbing of the toilet bowl and Navin's home—with its unleveled floors and peeling walls—was as ready as it ever would be to receive a respected guest.

"I have wine," Sid said as he walked through the door.

"Oh, thanks, Sid," Navin said.

"I thought we could drink this on the patio, but I suppose not."

"No, my patio is one of the twelve or thirteen steps out there."

Sid looked back to the staircase as if to imagine the two drinking wine shoulder to shoulder on a single step. "Inside will do!" Sid said. He took a few steps in and gave a judgeless look around. "What are you paying for this place?"

"Twenty-four-hundred dollars per month."

"That's not bad," Sid said. "A lifestyle choice?"

"Yes."

"So, where's this journal?" Sid asked.

"Seriously?" Navin asked. "You'd like to see it."

"Of course!" Sid said. "Of course, Navin."

As Navin retreated to his bedroom to retrieve the journal, Sid looked around Navin's sparsely decorated and furnished apartment—the sofa on which he sat; a coffee table; a small, square dining table; a television and some audio equipment; and a small portable CD player. Sid was content. His grin was unending, mostly because he realized even he had adopted technology more than Navin apparently had.

"Here it is," Navin announced, handing Steve Martin's journal over to Sid.

As Sid opened the book, Navin opened and poured the wine. Sid read from the first page he saw: "Steve Martin's journal: The comedian, the actor, the author." Sid let out an unguarded laugh.

"Pretty wild, huh?" Navin asked.

"And crazy," a normally unimpressed Sid said. He continued to flip the pages of the diary seeking something of interest. As he skimmed, Navin resisted his urge to list highlights of the journal. "Not very personal, is it?" Sid asked.

"No, not really," Navin said. "He's known for being intensely private, though."

"But this is *his* journal," Sid said. "Doesn't he share any secrets with *himself?*"

Navin laughed at the quip. "I guess not," he said. "Oh! See what you make of this . . ." Navin took the journal and opened it to the page that held the verse:

Eh! Star like charmer hated porno.
If wrong be, I am wanted and deplored.
The warm town inhabits, earns TV time.

Sid grinned. "What is it?"

"I don't know, but it's about the only intriguing thing that's in there," Navin said. "Besides what appear to be some very famous phone numbers and the like."

"You read Steve Martin's journal?"

"Well, I wasn't going to," Navin said. "In fact, it was important to me to not read any of it. Just return it to him. But I came across that verse and really wanted to know more about it, so I dug a little."

"And, nothing?"

"Not really," Navin said. "It's got a lot of data and general history in there, but nothing too personal."

"Does it even classify as a journal?" Sid asked.

"We'll say," Navin said.

"Pardon?"

"Oh, 'we'll say' as in 'we'll say so,' and so it is."

"Oh," Sid said slightly confused about Navin's stream of logic. "Well, he has very elegant handwriting. It's kind of big and loopy and confident."

"Well, I guess so," Navin said.

Sid flipped back to the page with the verse and read it aloud: "Eh! Star like charmer hated porno. If wrong be, I am wanted and deplored. The warm town inhabits, earns TV time."

"I have unwittingly convinced Geoff that the universe is at work, and this somehow is a direct message to me from Steve Martin," Navin said. "Well, maybe unknowingly, but because I found it and I'm lost and—"

"I don't think so," Sid said. "You found a journal in the snow. Big fucking deal. You know there is no god, right?"

"Oh . . . yeah," Navin said, now reminded with whom he was speaking.

Sid read the verse aloud a couple times, and then to himself. "Well," he said. "I don't know." And with that, he Frisbeed the journal to the now-barren coffee table.

"How was dinner?" Navin asked.

"It was fine," Sid said. "I think she still has a thing for me."

"Why do you say that?"

"She gave me a hand job under the table."

"Oh, well, *that's* telling. How can you be such a sophisticate and be such a scumbag?"

"It's a gift, Navin."

☙

Navin and Sid had walked to the beach and sat on a short cinderblock wall that rose above the sand. The night air filled with the two catching up on lost time. Navin had many questions for Sid and, uncharacteristically, Sid volunteered answers.

Sid had lost Amy, his wife of twenty-nine years, in an auto accident four-and-a-half years before. Their youngest children—a boy, Calvin, and a girl, Klay—had left home for college shortly thereafter. Lindsey—Sid and Amy's eldest, and Navin's schoolmate—had left home years before Amy's death for his career in political and cause-related fundraising.

Through the night, Sid told Navin that he had sold his thirty-four-hundred-square-foot house and moved into an eight-hundred-ninety-square-foot, downtown San Francisco condominium. He had sold most everything he owned—a beach home in Costa Rica, a ski retreat in Idaho, an apartment on Central Park West.

These days, he was a practicing dilettante as far as most things were concerned. Adventure traveling, however, was his new true passion, and a far cry from the five-star travel he enjoyed with his family before the accident. Sid told Navin about his personal reflection while roughing it through India and Turkey. In Africa, he found appreciation and gratitude. And, while lost in China, he found forgiveness and peace. As he updated his friend, Navin marveled that had there ever been anyone equipped to handle the tragedy of that ill-fated day four-and-a-half years before, it was Sid.

"And you have truly found peace?" Navin asked.

"I have," Sid said. "I think the key is that I always could take things as they were, enjoy them while I had them, and know that all things change, all things evolve," Sid said. "That put me in a spot to more ably deal with this thing. I am still often sad, but I find myself smiling about my Amy's life more than crying over her death."

"You embraced Amy," Navin confirmed.

"I did. There was no room in my love for her for my pride. Or being right. Being afraid to be wrong. We just were. And we still are. I let her make me happy. She let me do the same for her." Sid paused for a moment and beamed. "I talk to her each day."

"But what about that whole death-then-dirt thing?"

"She's within me, Navin, as long as I choose to embrace her. So, I still talk to her, and I open myself up to hearing her talk back." Sensing he had spent far too long talking about himself, Sid abruptly changed topics. "Do you ever hear from Suzy?"

"No, nothing," Navin said.

"Nothing?"

"Not a word. She just went."

"Miss her?" Sid asked poignantly.

"No. I don't, really. Maybe the idea." He paused and looked out to the familiar moonlit surf that had, of late, provided the soundtrack to his life. "I have lots of regret there, Sid."

"If you don't miss her then what is there to regret?"

"I didn't try," Navin said. "Like you said, there is no room in love for pride. For me, I didn't feel love because of pride."

The two paused for a moment. Sid feared that Navin may still have missed the point. He felt that had a relationship worked out with Jess or Audrey or anyone else, there would be no regret with Suzy. Navin's regret, he believed, was based on folding a winning hand. "You are bullshitting me now, my friend," he said. "And you are bullshitting yourself."

"How do you mean?" Navin asked.

"You have seller's remorse. You followed your heart at the time, or your mind, or both. You were not happy and you made a change. You were never compelled enough to call her back, were you?"

"No, but—" Navin began.

"But something is stuck in your craw," Sid finished.

"And it haunts you."

"Yes."

"Well?"

"Don't laugh," Navin warned, "but Steve Martin's journal did reach me for a reason. I am sure of it, but I don't know why."

"OK," Sid said. "I'll suspend disbelief for a moment. So what do you mean? Have you known this the whole time you have had it?"

"Yes! I just know it. There is a reason I have it, that I found it. I feel it. That I have to return it."

"Do you think this is why all the dreams and fantasies?"

"Yes."

"So you found this journal, and it is causing you to deal with something you locked away in a closet?"

"Yes."

Sid could see that Navin wanted to say something aloud. Sid remained silent to allow Navin to nurture his thought.

"You know when you're with someone and you can just communicate with a shared glance, or single line, or a smile?" Navin asked.

"Yes, I do."

"That was Suzy and me," Navin said as he began to smile fondly at a memory.

"I know," Sid said. "But it wasn't love, was it?"

"No," Navin said almost as a question. "I think it had been once."

"And?"

"Well, 'The Jerk,' the movie . . ."

Sid nodded.

". . . Was just one of those things couples have, you know?" Navin paused, seeking an example. "Like, any time one of us went on just a little too long about our day, the other would interrupt each sentence with 'You were?' or 'They did?' or 'He will?' Just asking mindless, confirming questions."

"Funny," Sid said. "I recall that scene."

"Yes, but I held onto that movie as an escape from real communication. When things got difficult, I could always throw a quote out and we would laugh, diffusing anything difficult."

"And it was extra funny because of your name."

"Yes," Navin said, and they smiled.

"You had a surefire way to run and hide," Sid said. "And she was able to help hide you."

"Yes, I suppose."

Sid looked intrigued with where this might be going. Navin's expression moved from the quick smile, to becoming glassy-eyed and oddly content, to glassy-eyed and uneasy.

"The last night I was with her," Navin said as he adjusted on the block wall, "we had sat without conversation for thirty minutes, maybe an hour. It was awkward and frustrating. The air felt like quicksand. She was flying away the next day. I think we both knew this was the last goodbye, but just didn't know how to do it, or if it was even something we wanted. Then she got up from the sofa and walked to the DVDs and found 'The Jerk.' She held it up and smiled—a smile I had never seen. It was nervous, tragic. It was desperate. Sad. She put the disc in the player and sat next to me. I never stopped looking at her. It was the saddest thing I've ever seen—more than anything in the news, on the streets, even sadder to me than Amy's death." Navin looked to Sid for his approval, and Sid gave a knowing and approving nod. "I am sure my expression matched hers. These expressions, I'm sure, were new to each of us.

"The movie began to play and there was no laughter. None. It was ceremonial. 'The Jerk' was what we knew together, that humor. Levity. And after all those years, even

'The Jerk' couldn't save us." Navin turned back to the sea.

"You didn't watch it?"

"Couldn't," Navin said. "Haven't since."

"How did it end?" Sid asked. "The night. How did it end?"

"I don't know," Navin said as tears streamed down his cheeks. "I don't remember. I just know I pulled the movie from the player. I don't even remember where I slept. The next thing I recall is dropping her at the airport terminal the next day, and her looking back over her shoulder at my car as she pulled her baggage behind her. And that was it. I never saw her again." Without a sob, tears streamed silently down his face.

The two sat in silence for a while. Sid was moved. Navin was introspective.

"Do you know why you hold onto that as a defining moment?" Sid asked.

"I don't know," Navin said. "Maybe because there were two people knowing where they wanted to go, but had no idea how to do it? Maybe because it defied logic. Maybe I should have tried harder? Maybe if I could just rewind back to that very moment, everything that followed might be different. Maybe because I saw desperation in her eyes, a look of helplessness.

Helplessness to help her. To help us."

"Maybe it's because you did truly love her."

"Maybe."

"Maybe you are taking too much blame for that look on her face."

"Maybe."

"Forgive yourself, Navin. If there is anything you think you could have done better, forgive yourself and turn the page. You will die soon. Start living."

"I am trying; I have been trying forever," Navin said.

"No, Navin, you have not."

☙

Navin walked into his bedroom and sat on the floor at the foot of his bed. He reached beneath and swept his arm from side to side. Touching nothing, he rolled onto his side and pressed his right shoulder and right temple to the floor. He spotted a shoebox and, with his left hand, reached and grasped it. He pulled it toward him and out from under the bed.

He straightened to a seated position on the floor and pivoted his body around to lean his back against the bed for support. He stretched his legs and crossed his ankles.

He placed the box on his thighs and opened the lid.

Photographs filled the box. There were images of a much-younger-appearing, much-thinner Navin. His hair was longer and blonder. He wore golf shirts tucked into ironed shorts. In some, he wore large sunglasses with deep lenses. His expression in all of the pictures was innocent and happy. Carefree and natural. Young and hopeful.

And there was Suzy—fresh, innocent, happy, and carefree. Humor lay behind her eyes in every photo, as did the exhilarating unease of being the subject matter of so many snapshots.

For her, he had no description. She was just "Suzy." Her hair was brunette, or blond, or strawberry. Her eyes were green, or hazel or gray. Her teeth were straight, or crooked or missing. He didn't really know. She was just "Suzy."

He flipped through the photos and each shot conjured a notion more than a memory. The backdrops were spectacular—the Amalfi Coast, the Greek Isles, Prague Castle.

When he had reached the bottom of the box, he found about a half-dozen ticket stubs for tourist attractions, concerts and movies. He tried to translate the languages on the stubs, and came to acceptable conclusions as to what they had done together—a tour of Pompeii, an afternoon Vivaldi performance in Venice, a "The Big Lebowksi" screening in Vienna.

And, as quickly as he paged through the prints and the tickets, he placed them back into the box. With no fanfare, he slid the box back under the bed and picked himself up off the floor. He walked to his kitchen, pulled a glass from the cabinet and filled it with water from the tap. Navin stared at the microwave clock but could not comprehend the time and, with one hand on his hip, took a drink.

He thought this is what Sid had meant when he spoke of Amy. The photos were not cause for trauma or regret. The box beneath the bed contained a celebration of Navin and Suzy's youth and coming of age. They were truly happy. And when they weren't any longer, then *they* weren't any longer. Navin was fond of Suzy and the time that was theirs. Together, they had had their time and place. It was wonderful. But it was over.

Navin guzzled the rest of the water and set the empty glass on the counter without breaking his gaze from the clock. He hooked his thumb through a belt loop and stood and thought of nothing for seemingly forever.

"I think I have it figured out!" Sid exclaimed into his phone as he walked through the Palm Beach International Airport terminal toward his departing flight.

"As to why I feel so bad about the night of 'The Jerk'?" Navin asked.

"No," Sid said. "Well . . . I don't have it all figured out. But I know what the verse is."

"Steve Martin's verse?" Navin asked. "What?"

"It's just a game, a folly. It's clever, but I think it means nothing."

"Sooo, you're not going to tell me," Navin said, recognizing Sid's penchant for embracing the moments in which he is smarter than the rest of the world. "You're just going to hang up now."

"No," Sid said laughing. "No, I don't have it all figured out and, quite frankly, because I know what it is I don't need to. But I will tell you where to look and you can decipher the rest."

"Decipher?"

"There is one phrase that sticks out like a sore thumb, random," Sid explained. "Notice it and ignore the rest and that will give you the next step."

"So it means nothing? The verse means nothing?"

"Well, I say that, but you be the judge," Sid said. "Just find the phrase that seems odd and try to see it in a different way. It popped out to me and I wasn't even trying. I just caught it funny. Have fun and goodbye. Oh and, Navin, be good to yourself."

Navin resisted the strong urge to tell him about the box of photos he went through the night before. The feeling of calm it brought him. The step that he might have taken to unlock so many other gates. He knew that Sid would have been proud. Even relieved. Certainly pleased. But he thought Sid deserved a pass. He had done enough. He could tell him later. And so, he simply smiled to himself.

"OK, Sid," he said. "Have a safe flight, and tell Amy 'hello' for me."

UNSCRAMBLED | 13

NAVIN LOGGED INTO his email account and saw more spam. The latest craze was the promise of nude celebrity photos. He deduced that this new offer was for anyone who took advantage of any boner prescription deals previously offered via email. Now, users would have new material for the magic pills that threatened a four-hour erection. This made sense to him in that anyone who would buy such a drug by responding to such an email probably also spends a lot of time at home alone and might need fresh inspiration. "Multilevel product diversification," Navin smiled. "Assist the spank, provide the bank. Brilliant."

He dumped the junk mail and logged onto one of his online dating accounts. "kittenluv" had tapped him. On this site, "tapping" someone was a quick way to express interest without having to reach out and say something via email. He read on kittenluv's profile that she had eight children and an annual income of between fifteen-thousand- and twenty-five-thousand dollars.

"lawlover02" had also tapped him. Her profile featured eleven photos—nine of which were of dogs and cats, one featured a lake, and the last a full-body shot taken from sixty feet away with a macro lens.

"MuchAMuNch" had actually sent an email, which stated that she very much liked African-American men, would like to become a United States citizen and found his profile to be hugely erotic. For starters, Navin was very much a Caucasian. The rest he heeded as warning signs.

Navin skimmed through profiles until the photo of a woman in a wheelchair caught his attention. Intrigued, he read her profile. Near the end of her description, she had written that she is every guy's dream because last-minute seats were always available in the handicapped section of the biggest sporting events. Navin chuckled. She was pretty. She had shortly cropped brunette hair, deep-brown eyes and high cheek bones. Her user ID, "Nikki," was void of any pretense. Navin began to read her profile a second time. In it, she dealt head on with her situation and explained the cause of her paralysis as not life-threatening. She wrote with an ease that defied the culture of the online dating scene:

> . . . I can only do my best and that is what I offer to the world. I hold onto nothing that is not mine . . .

He looked away from his computer. "This apartment's not mine," he said. "None of this is mine. That journal is not mine."

And so, without any further thought at all, he thanked Nikki with a wink at his screen, logged out of the site, and shut his laptop. He prepared an envelope for Steve Martin's journal by affixing four-dollars-and-thirty-eight-cents-worth of loose postage stamps he had in his kitchen. He addressed the outside with a Sharpie marker:

STEVE MARTIN
COMEDIAN, ACTOR, AUTHOR
HOLLYWOOD, CA
(OR SOME PLACE NEARBY)

Navin slipped on a pair of flip-flops and took the envelope to a curbside mailbox. As the envelope slid down into the darkness, he uncerimoniously said, "And that is that, then."

※

"Steve, your journal has been found and returned!" yelled a house servant as he ran into Steve Martin's home office. He waved the journal above his head. "It has been *found!*"

"Oh, ho ho, my!" Steve Martin exclaimed as he leapt from a plush, black-leather chair that sat behind his ornate, mahogany desk. "Are all the pages there?"

"I don't know, Steve!" the servant yelled as he reached him. "I don't know how many pages there were in it in the first place!"

"Well, of *course* you didn't!" Steve said. "If I had wanted to you to know, I would have *told* you!"

"But you didn't tell me!"

"No, I didn't tell you!"

"Because it was none of my business!"

"No!" Steve Martin affirmed. "It was none of your business!" He took the journal and flipped it open. He closed it and grasped a corner between his forefinger and thumb. He raised his arm and dangled the book. As it swung, Steve Martin peered toward it intently and, in a sudden revelation, his exuberance turned to scorn. "Wait a minute—my journal has been read!"

"How do you know?" the servant asked.

"How *couldn't* I know?" Steve Martin asked rhetorically. "Just, just, just . . . *look* at it!" Steve Martin held the stranger-read journal to the man's face.

The servant studied the journal as Steve Martin slowly turned it to show him all viewpoints. "I can see that, Steve," he said. "Someone has *read* your journal."

"Well, I understand the curiosity one might have about me," Steve Martin said. "But it's no excuse. If I am careless enough to drop this in the snow on a snowy Manhattan morning, or offer someone the chance to read my journal here in my office, no one should ever read my journal."

"I understand."

"Well, if my journal must have been lost for as long as it was, then I am hopeful that it spoke to its finder—spoke to him or her in such a way that it helped him or her explore him or herself; a self that has been riddled with self-doubt and low self-esteem; a self that has had many unanswered questions and many unresolved, deeply personal issues. And, I hope this journal has served to bring friends together and close old wounds. And, it is my hope that he or she can forget about him or her and enjoy the search for a new, more-meaningful him or her for he or she. And, I dream that someday this he or she will have a number of children with the new him or her, and he and she or him and her can enjoy the company of their children, and he and her with him, her and he, or he and she with her, him and her, or perhaps even *they* with he, he and he or her, her and her will enjoy their trips to Southern California and enjoy Knott's Berry Farm and Disneyland, as all the hims and hers visit the places that launched my career, which lead to me losing this journal, which helped the original he or she start anew." Steve Martin paused as he turned back to the servant. "*That's* what I hope."

"You're a good man, Steve Martin," the servant said.

"I know," Steve Martin said nobly. "I know."

From the pride that dripped from Sid's tone earlier in the day, it was clear to Navin that the verse was craftier than he had ever considered. He had, until now, only viewed the verse as the seeds to something more creative and artistic. He now sensed this was a code of sort. He pulled his coffee table toward the sofa and wrote the verse on piece of paper:

Eh! Star like charmer hated porno.
If wrong be, I am wanted and deplored.
The warm town inhabits, earns TV time.

Based upon Sid's cryptic phone call, Navin began to look the verse over to notice anything that did not fit in. He looked at structure. Everything seemed to match. Phrases such as "Star like," "If wrong be," "town inhabits," and "earns TV time" all seemed consistent. He knew nothing about poetry or its construction, so he tried to find a glitch in rhythm, but even then he didn't know what to look for. He reasoned that he had read and recited the verse so often, that if there had been any absence of rhythm his imagination now filled it in.

Frustrated, but still very excited, Navin changed his focus to the content. Words within the verse taken individually had no real meaning or context. "Charmer," he said aloud. "Porno, deplored, inhabits, TV . . . inhabits. In habits?"

A tapping pen to the paper timed his pondering of

the mixed use of "wanted" and "deplored." "Desire and regret," he said aloud. "Desire and regret," he repeated. "Sounds like my fucking life," he said.

Navin processed the mix of desire and regret until it led toward a dangerous path of self-exploration. "No," he said aloud. "Take care of yourself."

He began to search punctuation for clues. He scribbled through the "Eh!" and then "If wrong be." After a moment, he scribbled through "The warm town inhabits." He drew a line beneath the verse and rewrote the three phrases he had just marked through.

"Sid said something just leapt up and caught his attention," he whispered. "Is it visual?" He squinted his eyes and, once the scribbles dominated his attention, he tore the piece of paper from the tablet. On the next clean sheet he rewrote the verse as single lines in the new order he had created:

> *Star like charmer hated porno.*
> *I am wanted and deplored.*
> *Earns TV time.*
> *Eh!*
> *If wrong be,*
> *The warm town inhabits.*

The verse took the shapes of two pyramids stacked upon each other, with the top pyramid inverted and balanced on its point. Navin squinted again, and the white space drew his attention to the word "Eh." When Navin opened his eyes, "TV" came into focus.

"TV," Navin said. "Earns TV time," Navin said. "Earns TV time," he repeated. "Earns TV time . . . Earnstv time . . . Earn steve time . . . Steve time? Steve. Steve?" he grew excited. "Can't be this simple," he said.

He quickly crossed out the letters from the phrase that spelled "steve" and wrote the remaining letters below the verse:

A R N T I M

When he had finished, he froze, and it came to him almost instantly: "Martin!" he said. "Steve Martin! 'earns TV time' *is* 'Steve Martin!' Holy shit!"

He stood and walked a lap around his living room before sitting back down. Again he tore the top sheet of paper from the pad and rewrote the verse as it originally appeared. But this time, he unscrambled the last phrase to read "steve martin." He looked the verse over to find a demarcation that allowed for the fewest number of letters to unscramble. "If wrong be" was the obvious choice. He wrote the letters in reverse to change his point of view:

$$EBGNORWFI$$

He drew a deep breath and tapped his pen nervously to the paper. He thought that if the entire verse were an anagram, this might keep him busy for few days, weeks or months. If it wasn't an anagram, it might be a complete waste of time. "I wish I had worked the Jumble puzzles as a kid," he thought. "The cartoons just looked stupid."

He began to scribble different combinations of the letters on his tablet. After a few moments, he removed the tablet from the table and reclined back into his sofa. As he settled in, he began to pair letters that may work together. The letters N and G seemed an obvious pair, as did the letters E and W, or W and R. F and R jumped out at him, as well as B and R. He worked the combinations for about thirty minutes, until he combined the letters that formed the word "bow." And then, the puzzle was solved.

"It's one of his movies," he said. "Bowfinger."

DISCOVERY | 14

NAVIN SLID A folded piece of paper across to Geoff and placed it next to his cup of coffee. He gave a wry smile and rested his chin in his palm.

"So, this is it," Geoff said.

"Yup!" Navin said.

"What's written on this paper is why you haven't acknowledged me in three days?"

"Yup!"

"It's the meaning of the verse, isn't it?"

"Yup!"

"It's not the meaning of life, is it?"

"Nope!"

Geoff took a sip of his coffee, returned the cup to its saucer and picked up the paper. Navin's smile was wide, and he took a careless gulp of his coffee.

Looking at Navin, Geoff unfolded the paper, and looked down to read what was written:

Harris K. Telemacher, Parenthood.
Bowfinger, Dead Men Don't Wear Plaid.
The Man with Two Brains, Steve Martin.

"You're fucking kidding me," Geoff said.

"Nope!" Navin said.

"The verse meant nothing?"

"Don't think so!"

"Just a puzzle."

"Probably," Navin said. "I think it's meaningless."

"Do you think Steve Martin would have been so bored and self-indulged that he would have taken the time to do this?"

"No," Navin said, then paused. "Doesn't seem to fit, does it?"

"Not really," Geoff said. "So that's it, then."

"Yup!" Navin said while smiling. "That's it, then. Nothing left to figure out but my life."

"Well, you seem to be in good spirits."

"I think so. You know, we always see what we want to see. We remember things more fondly or more badly than the way they really were. We sort of bounce around until we get an explanation that matches what we want to hear or believe, and we accept it even if it's wrong. We don't want to change our belief system, our habits."

"Wow. Where did this come from?"

"I don't know, really. I just got to thinking about the key."

"The key?"

"I never told you about the key?"

"Nope."

"A key showed up near my bathroom vanity weeks before Audrey and I split. I left it there the whole time thinking I had put it there. Then, a couple weeks after we split up, I realized she had never returned her key to my apartment."

"She had, huh?"

"Yup. We were done weeks before; I just never got the hint that I was supposed to do it. I was supposed to end it."

"Geez. Calculating bitch, huh?"

"Calculating something," Navin said. "Talk about being blind for a goal. Just like this verse. I just didn't pay any mind to the key because it was a sign that contradicted what I thought I wanted. How many times when she described the only time she has ever been engaged did she refer to the 'big rock on her finger' in the first minute?"

"I don't know," Geoff said smartly.

"Oh," Navin laughed. "Well, too much. But I didn't want to notice. My mind was made up on how it should be. Like the key, or the verse, or whatever is happening at the McDonald's drive-thru, or whatever else, sometimes no matter how hard we try or what we think, it just isn't the way it's going to be. We just don't look, do we? But it's always right in front of us."

Geoff paused for a moment then made an annoyed face. Navin wondered if Geoff was bothered that he had made an important discovery.

"Fuck it, Navin," Geoff said.

Navin's hair rose on the back of his neck and without thinking he said, "Yes, Geoff. Fuck it."

"What?" Geoff said.

"No, you're right. Fuck it. Let's get out of here." Navin pulled the napkin from his lap and tossed it onto his plate, stood and walked out the door to the car. Geoff followed.

"Navin," Geoff said.

Navin stormed to Geoff's passenger door and waited for Geoff to push the button on his key to unlock it.

"Navin!" Geoff said. "What's up?"

"I need to get home."

Navin and Geoff sank into his car. Geoff turned the key, backed out of his parking space and turned onto the road. "What was that back there?" he asked.

Navin didn't answer. He just stared out the window as Geoff pulled to a red traffic signal. As he waited for a chance to make a right turn on red, he crept his car into the crosswalk.

"Navin," Geoff said.

Navin remained quiet.

"Navin!" Geoff said again, looking at him. When Navin turned to check for a clearing in traffic, he noticed a very overweight man on a motorized, four-wheel scooter driving straight for Geoff's door. "What's with this fuck?" Geoff asked as he reached for a balled tissue.

Navin broke his gaze and looked to see the man—dirty, with an unshaven neck beard, and angry—park the nose of his motorized chair just inches from Geoff's door. "I think you're in the crosswalk," Navin said.

"Yup, and this prick is going to let me know it." Geoff powered his window down. "Can you back up a little? I just don't want to hit you."

"You're in my crosswalk," the man said with both hands clutching his hand grips.

"Yes," Geoff said. "I know. I'm moving."

"You're in my crosswalk," the man repeated.

Navin, looking past the man into the oncoming lanes, said, "It's clear, Geoff. You can go."

"I'm not going until he backs up," Geoff said.

"You're not going to hit him," Navin said. "Just go."

"Don't park in my crosswalk," the man said.

"Go, Geoff," Navin said.

"And you're going to let me know it," Geoff said to the man without looking at him. The man stared at Geoff, and Geoff wiped his nose.

"Are you going?" Navin asked. "He's not in your way. You're clear."

Geoff and the man stared each other down as another car pulled up behind Geoff.

"Goddammit," Navin said, and unfastened his seatbelt and got out of the car. Geoff turned to watch Navin close the door behind him and walk around the front of the car to the man in the chair.

"OK, you fuck," Navin said to the man. "You've made your point, now let me make mine. This pussy behind the wheel here ain't budging because he is as lazy, unaccountable and entitled as you are."

"Whoa, pal—" the man started.

"No, whoa this," Navin said. "You wanted to start some shit and you did, and I'm finishing it." He turned to Geoff. "I'm fucking finishing it."

"Uh," Geoff muttered. "Navin—"

"Isn't this what you wanted?" Navin asked Geoff.

"No."

"It is," Navin said. "And so, here it is."

The driver of the car behind them blew his horn and leaned his head out the window to hear what was happening. "C'mon!" he yelled. A third car joined the line, and then two others.

"Get out of my way," said the man in the chair.

"Where the fuck you going?" Navin asked him. He turned back to Geoff. "Why have I brought you along, Geoff? Why? I am not letting you devalue my life anymore. I'm finding peace. You refuse to. Or you can't. Never have. I have been caught in your vortex since high school. I'm done. I am not watching you die anymore."

Navin turned and stormed back across the front of Geoff's car and began his walk over the bridge that led to his apartment and out of Geoff's life. "Where you going?" Geoff asked.

"I'm going on," Navin said without turning. "I'm starting my life."

Navin never turned back to see Geoff, as there was no Geoff to see. He never heard the horns that didn't blow from the traffic that queued behind a car that couldn't possibly exist. As he reached the span's summit, Navin smiled. He had just solved one of his most crippling problems: He would be free from this personality, and he would be free to live a life for his true self, and no other incarnation. He would now embrace his times as who he really was, and who he wanted to be. Through a chance find of a journal and a verse within, he discovered how to control the Geoff in his head, and notice the key to his vanity. He discovered how to count on his core. In a jarring awakening, Navin was free.

☙

Navin sat on his sofa with his laptop seesawing on his thighs and managed his email. Sid had written that he was about to leave for a South American tour. It was something he always wanted to do. Navin replied to Sid, and thanked him for the visit and resulting clarity. He typed out the solved verse and thanked him for his tip.

He surfed the Web to seek the news. Once again, the day's hard news was a repeat of yesterday's. A click or two later and Navin learned that Antony Brunopulcelli-Cabonolli had been traded one-for-one for Carmine Brunopulcelli-Cabonolli in the biggest NBA trade in recent memory.

Bonnie Jasper, one half of the former celebrity "it" couple "Bonzo," had been found with what was left of her fifty-two-year-old stepdaughter, Francis, in the basement of a Juarez, Mexico brothel, just across the border from El Paso, Texas. She had been tracked and found by cable-television celebrity-bounty hunter Shark. Once Shark returned Bonnie and Francis to the United States border, he was detained by Mexican authorities for violating his parole that stemmed from a conviction of eight years before. In the fall of 2005, he was found guilty of smuggling United States citizens into Mexico as illegal bounty hunters.

Navin then read that the *Budapest Sun*, an English-language newspaper, had published excerpts of two love poems written by the wife of the man who had been in a coma for nearly two decades. Hundreds of poems, along with scores of short stories, had been found in the ambulance in which the two were killed just moments following the husband's release from the hospital.

Upon the discovery of the wife's writings, officials in

Budapest moved swiftly to put forth a plan to commission a statue of the two. It would be erected on Margitsziget, an island on the Danube River that is known to locals for its serenity and romantic strolls. One official in Budapest referred to the tale as "a love story more true than anything ever known to this world." The local news media, the story said, had gotten behind the efforts to erect such a monument, and had declared that the Danube itself would be incomplete without it.

Navin, having for the first time chosen to know their names, wept joyfully.

CHANCE 15

NAVIN TOLD HIS date of how, just months before, he had found Steve Martin's journal; he was just weeks from moving from his near-beachfront apartment on Palm Beach to Manhattan; and about a Hungarian couple named Péter and Anna.

His date, a sophisticated red-haired woman named Kristen, played down her apparent family wealth and tried far too hard to speak at a level below her social footing. She spoke in rehearsed tones, drone-like at times. Her efforts to impress him with knowledge of all things common came off as pressed and contrived. She really liked him, it seemed, and worked hard to flatter him. But he had thought it all too familiar.

He had won her over effortlessly. Her laugh was genuine. Her gaze to him was real. Her body language was inviting. These were things that Navin, until now, had not noticed always happened on first dates. For the first time, he realized that he can charm, and he is interesting, and he didn't have to try so hard. But also for the first time, he realized that he wasn't going to buy into it. For the first time, he was noticing *his* reaction to *her*. For the first time, he didn't judge any relationship's potential on how she responded to him.

After dinner, Navin walked Kristen to her car and, in another first, made the move for the first kiss. Gently, he moved to kiss her on the cheek. "It was very nice meeting you," he said as he pulled away.

"You, too," she said bashfully.

He gave her a smile and turned to walk. He did not need to know if there would be a second date. He did not second-guess if she liked him. He had, at last, begun the process of truly finding somebody for him.

Navin reached his car and climbed inside. Along his drive home—and still dressed for his date in a current cut and wash of denim jeans, and a sharp black sports coat—he stopped at a Publix grocery store on the island to pick up some things for the rest of the week. He pushed his cart through the produce department and toward a small flower kiosk. He selected two bunches of daisies. These were cheap and would live just until he began packing his belongings to begin the move to New York City. As he placed them in his cart a young, fresh-faced woman with flowing black hair, riding her grocery cart like a kick scooter, breezed past him.

Unfiltered and without thought, Navin said, "Hey! You can't do that . . . this is Palm Beach."

The woman, in her late twenties, dismounted the cart and swung it around to take aim at him. She stepped her left foot on the bar between the two back wheels and pushed off with her right foot, then let her right leg hang as she rode to him. He cocked his head and gave an inquisitive smirk. She stopped her cart by lowering her right foot and asked, "What are you, PPD or something?"

"Huh?" he said. "Oh, Publix Pol–"

"Yeah," she grinned, "police."

He looked at her and was impressed with her giddiness. "Sorry to be so forward, but, are you drunk?"

"Ha!" she said. "Noooo. Not yet."

"Um, do your parents know where you are?" he asked sarcastically.

"Are you a prude or something?" she asked.

"Not really," he said. "I just think more people should shop the way you are shopping."

"I a-gree," she said. "Who are the flowers for?"

"Me."

"And you're dressed for a date?"

"Yup, but it's already over."

"It's only seven!"

"It was a happy-hour date. A first date. She needed an escape vehicle."

"So, you didn't get a chance to see where she lives?"

"You mean pick her up at her house?"

"Yeah! You have to be careful. Girls around here act like they got dough, and they don't. Or they do, and they have a big-time drug habit, or a really old husband. Or they do, and they're like sixty-two years old. Always make sure you look at their hands."

"What?"

"Money can buy you a new face, but they never fix the hands."

"Ahhh," he said as his head tilted back. "Excellent tip."

"So?" she asked.

"So, what?"

"Did you like her?"

"No, not in that way," he said. "But she liked me."

"Of *course* she did!"

Navin smiled and felt his ears blush. "Well, thank you."

"You sure picked out some crappy flowers," she said. "I mean, daisies are kind of nice I guess, but I think they're crappy. Crappy nice, I think. Yeah, that's what I think."

"Well, yes, I did, and they are, or . . . I don't know, I like daisies. But I'm moving from my apartment soon, so I don't want to—"

"Get roses!" she interrupted.

"Why? Do you like roses?"

"Yes, but they're not for me, they're for you, remember?"

"Yes, I do like roses," he said. His face lit up, and he rocked to the balls of his feet. "And you know what? I will. I'll buy myself roses."

The girl smiled and turned her cart to leave. "Just make sure they don't gyp you and put daisy stems on them!" she said.

Navin's arms dropped as he watched her scoot away. A shot flashed through his core. She had just passed the Marie Kimball test. "Hey, wait a minute!"

"What?" she asked, turning back around.

"Come here, let me see your hands," he said.

"Ohhh, ha!" the girl said as she came back. She framed her face with her hands. "No work done here!" she said as she shook her head and looked to the ceiling.

He beamed at her.

"I was looking for a ring," he said without the benefit of editing. He winced upon hearing the forwardness of his answer.

She gasped.

"What? I'm sorry, I didn't mean to . . .," he said. "So, you can blush!" he exclaimed, seeking immediate redemption. "That's nice to know."

"No, it's OK," she said smiling widely. Navin sensed he had charmed her, as she appeared to him as having grown shy and endearingly vulnerable.

He thought for a moment, and reached into his basket and smiled at the girl knowingly. In a single stroke up the flowers' stems, he stripped the blooms off the bunch of the daisies and handed her the remains. Clumps of flowers and petals dropped from his cupped hand to the grocery store's floor next to his near-empty shopping cart. "I got these for you—they *were* a couple of dozen of roses."

ತ

Navin awoke the morning after his impromptu first date with a girl he had met in the produce department at a nearby supermarket. He was fresh and awake. He could not lie still, but he could not get out of bed. He tossed in anticipation.

He could only think about how easy last night was. He knew very little about her, and there wasn't a memory that stood out above any other. He remembered how her black hair flared at the ends. He recalled the subtle streak or two of deep red strands, and how terrific he thought it looked. He vaguely remembered the smile she gave with only her eyes. The dimple in her chin. How she nearly snorted when truly tickled. How she was quick with her wit. He recalled the unrehearsed and eloquent way she opined, and the grace with which she used humor to acknowledge then escape any subject matter that threatened to get too serious. He remembered how her taunts were gentle and biting all at once, while his return volleys were taken by her with initial surprise and quick appreciation and shyness.

He remembered her blushing and rolling her eyes in awkward self-awareness when a gentleman approached their table and said that she was the most beautiful woman in the restaurant. And, he thought, she most certainly is that. Then he blushed with her.

He had a vague memory of her taking him by his hand as they walked to their cars. He remembered not thinking of a kiss, and that the hand was plenty enough. But he remembered nothing perfectly. Their improvisation had stoned him.

They had not shared a kiss, but still he walked on air. They had not had a drop to drink, but still the night was a blur—a wonderful, once-in-a-lifetime, magical, uneventful, simply boring, funny, happy, perfect blur. Nothing had happened in the day leading to that moment, and nothing had existed since. That perfectly nondescript, unmemorable night promised the world to them both. They were to be escorted into it by a jerk.

Navin grew anxious to confirm that he actually knew how to find her. He sprung from his bed and slid into the kitchen, where his phone was recharging on the counter. There, folded inside his phone case, was a note he barely remembered her writing:

Navin R. Johnson—tough luck on the name.
My number is in your phone.
Don't blow it. – Megan

He must have left his phone on the table when he went to the restroom the night before, he thought. He searched his phone's contact list and found "MEGAN :)"

and a phone number. He smiled and walked to the front door and looked out his window past the neighbor's house for his skinny view of the sea.

Slightly wired and needing time to determine what to do next, he opened his apartment's door and went downstairs to get the mail. He thumbed through the letters as he climbed the steps and noticed a photocopied note on powder blue paper. The note said that someone in the Palm Beach zip code had anonymously returned a piece of personal property to a celebrity. A letter awaited that person at the Palm Beach USPS branch office.

"Holy shit!" Navin said, and he ran to his bedroom to get dressed to run to the post office.

⚜

"And who did you mail this piece of property to?" a postal service employee asked from behind the counter.

"Steve Martin," Navin said.

"And what did you return to him?" she asked.

"His journal," Navin said.

"Then this must be yours," she said as she reached below the counter to hand Navin a letter-sized envelope. "We've gotten ten Donald Trumps, four Jack Nicklauses, and a million any-Kennedy-you-can-name. So this must definitely be yours."

The woman handed the envelope to Navin and asked him to sign for the parcel. He did, thanked her, and left the post office.

❦

To whom this might interest:

The journal that was so carefully addressed to me was not mine. I do very much appreciate the effort you took to return it to me, even if it did essentially involve putting my name on an envelope above the word "California" and wishing it the best of luck.

In an odd twist of serendipity, my publicist had been contacted by an aspiring writer, who had claimed to lose a similar journal. As it turns out, the journal that was missing was, in fact, a simple notebook full of minor research he was doing in preparation for a screenplay.

The screenplay is to be about a man who had many dreams about me, and these dreams helped him face and deal with his own demons. A really interesting idea, I think, but I'm not sure if it has legs.

Anyway, this is the book you had sent to me. The notebook has been returned to its owner thanks to your anonymous effort.

At any rate, I have dictated this letter to my assistant in hopes that it reaches you. Though the book was not mine, I do truly appreciate your effort to return something that might have been. So for the thought, thank you.

Please tell others how thoughtful I am.

Yours,
Steve Martin

Navin smiled and read the letter again. He paced the living room of his apartment once or twice. He read the letter a third time.

He went to the kitchen and retrieved his phone. He flipped it open and pressed a couple buttons and held the phone to his ear. As he waited for an answer, his eyes scanned the walls and ceiling of his apartment, but he saw nothing.

"Hello?" answered a voice Navin hardly knew.

"Megan, it's Navin."

"Navin!" Megan said. "Hi! You didn't lose the number, did you?"

"No," Navin said. Though he laughed, the nuance of her joke was lost on him. "Guess what!"

"What?" Megan asked.

Navin looked to the microwave clock. The time was 10:10.

ACKNOWLEDGEMENTS

Writing is like smoking; it forces friends to breathe in whatever is coming out—whether they want to, or not. Endless thanks (and apologies) to the pre-readers for their notes; Chris English, Zoe English, Beth Lano, Steve Chapman, Ryan Donally, Terry Newcomb, John Padon, Andy Crossley, Teri Riley, Jonathan Fleisig, Steve Flynn, Lyndsi Erickson, Rachel Wright, Tera Black, and my brother, Allen.

A special thanks to Lisa Ferguson for going above and beyond, for her enthusiasm, and her encouragement throughout the inevitable second-guessing.

To John Katsilometes, Ron Kantowski, Tony Moreno, Jeff Molitz, Travis Keys and Beth Lano (yet, again), thank you for your support, advice and resources; and thanks to Bob Hill for being a very early personal influence, and for having a catch along the third base line.

Puggle Kimi Räikkönen remained mostly calm throughout the process, so, "Good girl and I owe something you think is bacon," and thanks to Bruce Springsteen for using the name *Billy* in all those songs.

Thank you, Erica, for your excitement and encouragement to get to "The End."

And thank you, Loretta, for your wit—and for laughing at mine.

CPSIA information can be obtained at www.ICGtesting.com
Printed in the USA
LVOW13s1453081013

356005LV00001B/101/P

9 780989 682107